What on eart

Charlotte became worried. She couldn't share her home with Oliver Tennant, of all men.

Why not? an inner voice demanded acidly. Do you really have so little faith in your own self-respect?

"You're so sensible, Charlie," her ex-fiancé had complained. "Always doing the right thing." And though she'd realized their engagement had been a mistake, there was still a small raw place inside that hurt from time to time; it was hurting now.

Do you honestly believe, the inner voice went on, that just because you'll be living under the same roof, you're likely to do something stupid, like...?

Like what? she asked herself, bitterly. Like fall in love with him? Of course she wouldn't; she was far too sensible for such folly.

PENNY JORDAN was constantly in trouble in school because of her inability to stop daydreaming—especially during French lessons. In her teens she was an avid romance reader, although it didn't occur to her to try writing one herself until she was older. "My first half-dozen attempts ended up ingloriously," she remembers, "but I persevered, and one manuscript was finished." She plucked up the courage to send it to a publisher, convinced her book would be rejected. It wasn't, and the rest is history! Penny is married and lives in Cheshire.

Penny Jordan's striking mainstream novel, *Power Play*, quickly became a *New York Times* bestseller. She followed that success with *Silver*, a story of ambition, passion and intrigue.

Penny's latest blockbuster, *The Hidden Years*, is now available wherever paperback books are sold.

Books by Penny Jordan

HARLEQUIN PRESENTS
1282—BEYOND COMPARE
1297—FREE SPIRIT
1314—PAYMENT IN LOVE
1324—A REKINDLED PASSION
1339—TIME FOR TRUST
1353—SO CLOSE AND NO CLOSER
1369—BITTER BETRAYAL
1388—BREAKING AWAY
1404—UNSPOKEN DESIRE

HARLEQUIN SIGNATURE EDITION
LOVE'S CHOICES
STRONGER THAN YEARNING

Don't miss any of our special offers. Write to us at the following address for information on our newest releases.

Harlequin Reader Service
P.O. Box 1397, Buffalo, NY 14240
Canadian address: P.O. Box 603,
Fort Erie, Ont. L2A 5X3

PENNY JORDAN

---

rival attractions

Harlequin Books

TORONTO • NEW YORK • LONDON
AMSTERDAM • PARIS • SYDNEY • HAMBURG
STOCKHOLM • ATHENS • TOKYO • MILAN

Harlequin Presents first edition December 1991
ISBN 0-373-11418-4

Original hardcover edition published in 1990
by Mills & Boon Limited

RIVAL ATTRACTIONS

CHAPTER ONE

As CHARLOTTE turned the corner and swung her ancient Volvo estate car into the square which, when not in use as a market, served the town as its most central parking area, she cursed under her breath.

The car park was full; of course, it would have to be when she was running late like this. Not that Paul would mind. But she did. She hated it when she found herself running behind schedule.

Today had been an exceptionally busy day—one of her busiest perhaps since she had taken over the running of the estate-agency business her father had established here in this small Lincolnshire country town, almost six years ago now.

Initially, when her father had first become ill, she had just stepped in on a temporary basis, but as the months had passed and it had become clear that her father was never going to be well enough to return to work, she had unwillingly given in to the emotional pressure he had put on her to give up her plans for living and working in London, independent of his rather dominating personality and the confines of a small country town where everyone knew everyone else's business.

Her father hadn't been an easy person to live with, and he had certainly not been easy to work for. Although nominally Charlotte was in charge of the business, her father had demanded a full nightly report on everything that was happening, often criticising her to the point where she had had to fight to hold on to her temper, and to remind herself that he was a very sick man, who had to be humoured and cosseted. Now her father was dead, and there was really no reason why she shouldn't sell up and leave. That was the trouble with growing older, she reflected, as she searched the square for a parking place. You became reluctant to make changes. The impetus which would once have taken her back to London was gone; she had become too used to small-town life and the last six years had developed in her a reluctant loyalty to the business which her father had founded. She liked dealing with people. She enjoyed the independence of being her own boss, of being able to make her own innovations and alterations. In the last few months of his life, her father had been unable to take any interest in the business whatsoever, and since his death she had experienced an odd disorientating sense of inertia, which made her reluctant to make any radical changes in her life.

Let's face it, she told herself, you've become a small-town person... set in your ways... used to a certain routine.

She was almost twenty-eight years old, mature enough to appreciate what she could and could not have from life.

Ahead of her she saw brake lights illuminate one of the parked cars. Someone was leaving the car park. And then, as the driver started to reverse, she saw the car on the other side of the car park, patiently waiting to reverse into the soon-to-be-empty spot. Only, oblivious to the waiting car, the one pulling out was reversing in its direction—leaving the emptying space unprotected. If she was quick, she could drive straight into it. She gnawed on her bottom lip, knowing that the other driver would have every right to be furious, but telling herself virtuously that on this one occasion her need was very much the greater.

She had to see Paul to settle the last of her father's financial affairs. The rest of her week was fully booked up. Their hitherto very quiet part of the country was suddenly being invaded by city dwellers in search of rural escapism. Over the last month she had been besieged with enquiries from Londoners wanting to explore the possibility of moving out to the country. While this was good for business, it had its negative side. The town was only small; house prices were shooting up, which meant that local young people, first-time home buyers, and those elderly couples who had lived in tied properties throughout their working lives, were now being priced out of the property market.

Charlotte was still frowning over this as she quickly nipped into the now-vacant parking space.

If she was quick, she would be out of her car and on her way to Paul's office on the other side of the square before the affronted driver could object to her stealing of his or her spot.

Slightly shamefacedly, she opened her car door and got out.

She was wearing her normal working uniform of a long-line box-pleated skirt, a shirt, and a thick woollen jumper over the top of it. In the back of the Volvo were her wellies and Barbour—essential items for life in the country, especially when her job took her to outlying properties to do valuations. Spring had been slow in coming this year, and Charlotte had long ago discovered that short skirts and high heels, elegant though they might look, were not very practical garb when it came to crawling around measuring floors and walls.

Had anyone asked her to describe her own looks, she would have said offhandedly that she was a little over average height, probably slightly too thin; that her face, with its high cheekbones and thick, straight eyebrows, was not softly feminine in the way that men liked; that her shining waterfall of glossy dark hair lacked sensual allure; and that her eyes, grey rather than blue, saw things a little too clearly to appeal to the majority of the male sex.

Her mother had died when she was five years old; her father had not remarried, and he had brought Charlotte up on his own, never really allowing her to forget that she was not the son he would have preferred, and yet somehow underlining at the same time that she was not the kind of feminine, appealing daughter he would have liked.

Because of this, she had grown up with a direct, uncompromising manner towards other people of both sexes, and a protective, almost stark belief that she was not the kind of woman who was likely to appeal to men, and so, for that reason, she might as well learn to be independent and like it.

As the years had passed and she had seen some of the marriages of her schoolfriends disintegrate under the pressures of modern life, she had watched, helped and commiserated as those friends had rebuilt their broken lives, and she had wondered if, after all, she was not better off than them. She might never have known the joys of loving and being loved, but neither had she experienced the pain of committing herself to another human being only to have that commitment rejected.

She had seen too often what it did to her sex when that rejection came—how hard it was for a woman who based her whole identity and life on the man she shared that life with to establish a separate, independent identity and life when the relationship was over.

Women were their own worst enemies, she thought. They loved too generously, made themselves too vulnerable. Men seemed to have an inbuilt ability to protect themselves from the kinds of hurts that women suffered. She had lost count of the number of times she had seen couples she had thought of as being happily married break up, the man walking away to a new life, leaving the woman broken-hearted, alone, often with enormous emotional and financial problems to cope with—not to mention the children of the marriage.

Charlotte was an intelligent woman; she knew that there were men who suffered just as much as women, but by and large the ratio of suffering seemed to her to be weighted far too heavily in her sex's direction.

She had been engaged once, briefly, but, when her father had become ill and she had had to return home, Gordon had become petulant and irritable, resentful of her decision to put her father's health first. When he had given her an ultimatum—her father or him—she had seen quite clearly how their lives together would be, how she would eventually become the victim of his desire to dominate their relationship emotionally.

There had been no passion in their relationship, and their decision to end their engagement had been mutual. It had been something they had drifted into as colleagues at the large estate agency where they both trained. If secretly she had hoped that he would soften towards her, and accept her need to help her father even though she would rather have been with him, she hardened her thought against that vulnerability when their engagement ended.

Since then there had been no man in her life. If challenged she would have said that men found her intimidating rather than alluring, and that she preferred it that way. Living in a small town as she did, with a position to maintain in the community, brief affairs, sexual flings, even the odd innocent moment of dalliance were not things that could be kept secret, and since she had no desire to find herself the object of local speculation, knowing how difficult it had originally been to get people to take her seriously in her business role, she had abandoned without too much reluctance the idea of having any kind of relationship with the opposite sex.

Her life was busy and fulfilled. She had good friends, an interesting career, her independence, both financial and emotional, and if ever there were times when, while cuddling a friend's child, the soft, warm body weakeningly close to her own, she ached for a child of her own, she only had to remind herself of the traumas she had seen her friends go through at the hands of those same men, who had given them their children, to make herself realise that the price she was paying for her independence, while high, was perhaps worthwhile.

She would have liked children. She enjoyed their company, their conversation, their innocence and naturalness, but Little Marsham was not the kind of place where one could fearlessly and modernistically announce that one was going to become a single mother. No, for Charlotte, her present way of life was the best way: single and celibate.

She pulled a face to herself, and then realised that her shortest route to Paul's office was straight across the car park in front of the driver whose parking spot she had appropriated.

It was a large dark blue Jaguar saloon car, driven by an equally impressive male, of the type most likely to cause susceptible female hearts to beat faster.

One quick guarded look told her that he was tall, dark-haired and with the kind of raw maleness that his expensive suit and white shirt did little to conceal, and that his eyes were almost the same colour as his car!

Reminding herself that she was the kind of woman who was not affected by such physical manifestations of male sensuality, Charlotte hastily averted her eyes from the car and its driver. The faint heat she could feel burning up under her skin was due to the guilt she felt at pinching his parking spot, she told herself.

She had only glanced briefly at him, but in that short space of time she had registered the fact that he was regarding her with a certain wry irony that told her he knew quite well that *she* was the one who had deprived him of his parking place.

She told herself that if she hadn't done so she would probably still have been driving around, making herself later than ever for her appointment. She was going to a dinner party tonight; she still had to do her monthly supermarket shopping; she had some reports to dictate on the properties she had seen today.

The influx of new, wealthy London-based buyers had seen an increase of property on to the market, especially those situated outside the town—often large and rather dilapidated houses with owners on the verge of retiring, who were looking for something smaller and more economical to run. Rather as she ought to be doing, she reminded herself. The house her father had bought when he first moved to the area over thirty years ago had originally been a vicarage. Several miles outside the town, on the edge of a small village, it was a rambling, draughty place with an enormous garden, and far too many rooms for one person.

She ought to sell it now, while the market was buoyant, buy herself something smaller and invest what was left. She had not had a particularly happy childhood; there was no reason why she should feel that she ought to keep the house. It should be filled with a family, with children, dogs, and perhaps a pony in the paddock. She could sell it tomorrow and virtually ask her own price, despite the fact that the central heating was fired by an ancient and temperamental boiler, the rooms all needed redecorating, and the garden was like a wilderness.

So why hadn't she done so? Shaking her head at her own impracticality, she crossed the road and hurried into the building which housed her solicitor's office.

Like her, Paul was the second generation of the family business. He was three years her senior, and they had known one another virtually all their lives. At one time Paul had tried to date her, but it had been just after she had come home, still sore from her broken engagement, too drained by the hard work of adjusting herself to living at home with her father. They had remained friends, though, and she liked Paul's wife Helen very much indeed.

Paul greeted her affectionately when his secretary showed her into his office, telling her it didn't matter when she apologised for being late.

'Business good?' he asked her when she was sitting down.

'Pretty hectic.'

'Mm... Recently there seems to be a lot of outside interest. That should be good for you.'

Charlotte pulled a face.

'Yes, financially, but there are broader implications. I had John Garner and Lucy Matthews in the other week. He and Lucy are getting married this summer. They've been looking for a suitable house locally for months. John will take over his father's farm eventually, but there isn't room there for them to move in. John's the eldest; there are four other children still at home. Naturally he and Lucy want a place of their own, but we just haven't had anything they can afford. His wages are low, and Lucy doesn't earn much either.'

'Can't one of the farm buildings be converted into something for them?'

'Not without planning permission, and you know how keen the local council is on keeping new building to a minimum. In theory that's something I approve of, especially when it comes to new estates, but...'

She gave a small shrug and, watching her, Paul said gently, 'The trouble with you, Charlie, is that you take things too much to heart.'

She flushed a little. Everyone who knew her well called her by the diminutive name she had been given while still at school—another sign that she was lacking in femininity, she reflected wryly.

Treacherously her thoughts slid to the driver of the blue Jaguar car; she'd bet that the women in his life weren't given boyish nicknames.

Instantly she was furious with herself. What on earth had made her think that? Was she so very predictable after all? she asked herself scornfully. A brief glimpse of a handsome face, an awareness of the scrutiny with which a pair of dark blue eyes were studying her face, and suddenly she was seeing herself through those blue eyes and finding herself lacking.

She tried to concentrate on what Paul was saying.

'It will mean extra business for me, but, of course, it's bound to affect you.'

She tensed, suddenly realising what he was talking about.

It had been just after her father's death that she had first heard the rumours that a new estate agent was contemplating opening up in the area. The influx of newcomers into the area had obviously attracted the attention of people looking for new business activities. Over recent months a rash of expensive small shops supplying luxury goods had opened up in the town; the owner of the local garage had been bought out, and the newcomers had knocked down the old building and rebuilt a large custom-designed showroom, which was now filled with shiny expensive cars, and small, prettily covered four-wheel-drive dinky toys with exotic and unpronounceable names.

It was a long way from the old days when Fred Jarvis supplied petrol, did repairs and maintenance, and could when pressed find you an ancient but roadworthy Land Rover.

Perhaps she ought to have been more prepared for competition in her own field, but she had been so exhausted by the effort of nursing her father through the final weeks of his illness that, when she had heard the gossip about the new estate agency opening up in the town, she had merely absorbed it without thinking about its impact on her own life.

Now she said evenly, 'Well, there's enough business for both of us.'

She didn't add that she suspected the newcomer would be after a quick killing, that he would take advantage of the surge of buying and selling, no doubt taking the cream off the top of her business with the larger, more expensive properties.

Paul was looking dubious, and Charlotte could guess what he was thinking. The townspeople were set in their ways, traditionalists in the main like her father; they had dealt with her when they had had no choice, but now, with a new agency opening up, no doubt run by a man, would they still give her, a woman, their business?

'At the moment, yes, but when this boom is over...'

'When it's over he'll probably close up his office and move away again,' Charlotte told him shortly. 'After all, from what I've heard this office is only going to be one of several.'

'I believe so, yes,' Paul agreed.

Charlotte sighed, knowing all that he didn't want to say. She knew quite well how these modern agencies worked: brash, pushy, promising the earth, persuading people into taking on much larger mortgages than they could afford, and taking a commission on selling the finance to them. That was not the way she did business.

Paul was speaking again.

'I'm surprised they didn't approach you with an offer to buy you out.'

'It's just as well they didn't. I wouldn't have sold. Have I signed everything now?' she asked him, changing the subject. She hated being the object of the concern and almost pity of her friends, who all seemed to assume that she was bound to lose out to the newcomer. She was proud of the way she ran her business—her values might be old-fashioned, but she intended to hold on to them. If the arrival of the newcomer meant that she had to scrap the plans she had been making for expanding, then at least no one but herself knew of those plans.

'I suppose you're going to the Jameses' tonight?' Paul asked when he had checked that she had signed everything.

Charlotte nodded and grimaced. 'Yes, but I'm not looking forward to it. I like Adam, but Vanessa isn't really my type.'

'Nor mine,' Paul agreed. 'She's a bit of a man-eater.'

Adam and Vanessa James were the local high-fliers. Adam was a quiet, studious man in his late thirties whose innovative skill in the world of computers had led to his establishing a very successful business. They had moved into the area five years ago, buying a large Victorian house on the outskirts of the same village as Charlotte's father's house.

Charlotte had always felt that in some way Vanessa resented her, although she could not see why. By her own lights Vanessa had everything she wanted from life: a wealthy, generous husband, who turned a blind eye to her determined flirtations with other men; a superb home, on which no expense had been spared; two quiet, dull children, who spent most of their time away at boarding school. Add to that the frequent shopping trips to London, their attendance at all the major events of the social calendar, holidays in the Caribbean in winter, and other far-flung exotic and fashionable spots in summer, and it was difficult to understand the resentment that Charlotte always felt emanating from Vanessa. What had she got that Vanessa could possibly envy?

Vanessa was a small, delicate blonde with a façade of pretty-prettiness that set Charlotte's own teeth on edge; they were poles apart in every way there was.

In Vanessa's shoes, Charlotte doubted that she would have asked her to her dinner party, but Vanessa always made a point of including her in her invitations, and then always put her back up by making derogatory comments either about her single status or what Vanessa liked to call her 'feminism'.

Given free choice, Charlotte would not be attending tonight's dinner party, but she liked Adam and felt sorry for him, and it was the kind of affair that would be bristling with important business contacts. She was attending in her role as local estate agent, that was all, and she would much rather have spent the evening getting some of her paperwork out of the way.

The car park was almost empty when she returned to her car. She noticed guiltily that the dark blue Jaguar was parked a few spaces away, mercifully without its driver.

As she drove homewards, perhaps because of Paul's comments, her mind was on the new estate agency opening up in competition to her. She had told Paul that there was enough business for both of them while the boom lasted, and that she suspected that once it was over the newcomer would close his office and go elsewhere. These new high-powered agencies weren't interested in local communities and small business, they wanted quick high profits, so in the long term, if she could just survive, she felt she had nothing to fear.

None the less she did feel slightly uneasy as she drove back to the village. From being bright and unclouded, the future had suddenly become threateningly overcast. As she turned into the long gravel drive to the house, the knowledge that there was no one inside waiting for her, no one with whom she could share the burden of her doubts and fears, depressed her.

She and her father had not been close, but she did miss him. They had not always agreed, but before his illness had become too much for him, they had been able to discuss the business. She had friends, of course, good ones, but her father's teaching and her own natural caution inclined her away from discussing her problems with them. She was more used to the role of confidante, that of receiving confidences rather than giving them.

Her telephone was ringing as she walked into the kitchen. She picked up the receiver, and frowned a little as she recognised the still girlish voice of Sophy Williams.

Sophy had been widowed tragically six months previously. Her husband had been killed in a road accident. At only twenty-three he had not thought to carry adequate insurance on his own life, and, although their small house was now Sophy's outright, with two small children to support and no proper income she had no idea how she was going to find the money to run the house and feed and clothe the children and herself. Although she didn't want to do so, she was beginning to feel she would have to sell her home and move in with her parents.

Promising to visit her the following day, Charlotte was still frowning as she replaced the receiver.

Although luckily she had not as yet said anything to Sophy, Charlotte had been considering offering her a part-time job. She could do with an assistant to help her. Sophy's twins were only three years old, but Sophy's next-door neighbour in the small row of terraced houses where they lived was a retired schoolteacher, who Charlotte suspected would be only too happy to look after the children for her for a small part of each day. It had been her intention to propose to Sophy that she made what outside visits to potential clients were necessary during the hours that Mrs Meachim looked after the twins, and that all her paperwork could then be done from home, so that she was there with the twins for the rest of the day.

At this stage she could not afford to pay Sophy a great deal, but she would train her properly and, once the twins were at school, she envisaged taking Sophy on on a more full-time basis.

Sophy was a touchy, proud girl, all too well aware that her parents had not approved of her marrying so young. As she had confided miserably to Charlotte, the only option she seemed to have was to sink her pride, sell the house and move back in with her parents who had grudgingly offered her and the twins a home. Charlotte knew quite well that if Sophy thought for one moment that she was offering her a job out of pity she wouldn't take it. She had hoped to convince the younger girl that, with the sudden property boom, she desperately needed more help than that provided by Sheila Walsh, who ran the office for her, but now that she was facing competition from another agency Charlotte was not sure that Sophy would be so easy to deceive. She was an intelligent girl.

Tomorrow Charlotte hoped to dissuade her from putting her house on the market. She knew how much Sophy prized her independence. Her parents' home was immaculate, and Mrs Sellars was particularly fussy about both the house and the garden. She would not enjoy having a pair of mischievous three-year-olds permanently about the place.

Sophy had said as much herself, and then added that, despite her own reluctance to accept her parents' offer, she didn't see that she had much alternative. She had no mortgage to pay, but no money coming in either. With what she would make on the sale of the house, she would be able to invest money for the twins' future, and living with her parents she would have very little outgoings.

Tomorrow, hopefully, Charlotte would be able to persuade her to reconsider, knowing as she did all the doubts Sophy had about moving back with her parents.

A glance at the kitchen clock warned Charlotte that it was time for her to go upstairs and get changed.

The kitchen had changed very little over the years since her mother's death. In fact, nothing in the house had changed. There had been times when she had tried to persuade her father to redecorate and refurnish, but he had obstinately refused to do so.

Now the house was hers, she recognised, and, looking around the bleak, dull kitchen, she acknowledged that it was no wonder she found it unappealing to come back to.

If she were selling it for someone else, she would be forced to tell the owners it had very little buyer appeal, that it might be structurally sound, waterproof and weatherproof, but that it lacked warmth, and the kind of ambience that drew prospective purchasers.

Her father hadn't been a wealthy man, but he hadn't been poor either. Charlotte had been a little surprised to discover how much money she had inherited, quite apart from the business. By rights she ought to sell this house and buy something much smaller, more easily run—something more suitable for a career woman who had very little time to spend on caring for her home.

She couldn't sell it in its present unappealing state, she decided grimly, mentally comparing it to the homes of her friends. She had several friends who had performed wonders with houses initially far more unprepossessing than hers. She would have to ask their advice. She certainly didn't have the time herself to search for fabrics and wall coverings, to engage workmen and choose fitments...

But she might have, if the new agency took too much of her business. A cold finger of apprehension seemed to touch her spine, a tiny icicle of fear. There was enough business for both of them, surely? She couldn't let her father down by losing everything he had worked so hard for. Shrugging her disquiet aside, she headed for the stairs, making a mental decision to lose no time in seeking the help of her friends in revamping the house.

It was almost as though in making that decision she was forcing herself to believe that, despite this newcomer, her own agency would survive. She *had* to have that belief in herself, she acknowledged wryly as she opened her bedroom door, because there was certainly no one in her life to have that faith in her.

Disliking her mood of self-pity, she grimaced mockingly at her reflection in the mirror. What was the matter with her? She had looked into a pair of navy-blue eyes and suddenly become aware of the fact that she was a woman and very much alone. Was she going through some sort of emotional crisis? Some sort of watershed? She was perfectly happy with her life the way it was, for goodness' sake. The owner of the blue eyes was not even the kind of man who appealed to her. He had been too good-looking, for one thing...too assured...too male.

A tiny shiver touched her, exposing a hidden raw spot of unhealed pain. She was well aware that such a sensual man would never be attracted to a woman like her, that he would not find her feminine and soft enough, that he would be antipathetic to her independence, her staunch determination to be seen as a human being and not a woman.

No, he was the kind of man who gravitated more naturally to the Vanessas of this world, to the sugar and spice of the softness that in reality cloaked a sharp hardness that was far more dangerous than her own gritty independence. At least she was honest, and made no attempts to conceal what she was.

The Vanessas of this world pretended to a vulnerability they did not actually possess, using it to pander to the male ego. By rights she ought to despise both them and the men who were stupid enough to fall for their deceit. Angry with herself, she turned away from the mirror and hurried into her bathroom.

If she was not going to be late, she'd better shower and wash her hair.

CHAPTER TWO

CHARLOTTE was late. The Volvo had been reluctant to start. It had originally been her father's car, and when she had come home, giving up her job and her life in London, she had automatically started using it.

Somehow or other she had never got round to replacing it, but now she recognised, as she drove skilfully towards the Jameses' house, that she was going to have to think about doing so.

She thought enviously about the sleek dark blue Jaguar, and then dismissed this fantasy from her mind. What she needed was something sturdy and sensible, not something glamorous and powerful.

When she reached the Jameses' house it was to find the circular drive already packed with parked cars. Under the illumination of the expensive reproduction lights, the lawn looked as smooth and immaculate as a newly laid carpet. The gardens to the rear of the house had, only last summer, been expensively and extensively redesigned by a fashionable London firm; the gravel beneath the Volvo's wheels had been specially chosen to tone with the stone of the house.

Charlotte knew all these things because Vanessa always made a point of announcing and describing at great length whatever renovations she was currently engaged in. As she climbed out of the Volvo,

Charlotte wondered why it was that she allowed the other woman to needle her so much.

It was Adam who opened the door to her knock. He gave her a warm smile as she stepped inside, and kissed her on the cheek. Vanessa appeared in the hallway just as he was doing so, her eyes sharpening as they studied the warmth in her husband's eyes as he welcomed their last guest.

'Charlie. At last. In a rush, were you?' Vanessa asked sweetly as she hurried her into the drawing-room, adding in a light and very audible voice, 'You must come with me the next time I go to London. I know a couple of places where they specialise in fitting difficult figures.'

Charlotte knew that her black velvet skirt was out of fashion. She did not have many evening clothes, having limited opportunity to wear them, but Vanessa's gibe about her appearance had been bitchily unnecessary. She might not have Vanessa's small, curvaceous femininity, but there was nothing 'difficult' about her figure. She was on the thin side, yes, but fitted easily into standard size ten clothes and never had the slightest trouble buying things off the peg, which was probably more than could be said for Vanessa, who seemed to purposely choose clothes which drew attention to her small waist and disproportionately full breasts.

Charlotte knew it was illogical to suddenly become aware of the fact that *her* breasts were perhaps a little on the small side; it wasn't something that had ever particularly bothered her, apart from once or twice during their engagement when Gordon had admiringly commented on the more generous charms of other women, but, illogical or not, she discovered that she was suddenly hunching her shoulders, as though trying to conceal her upper body from any curious glances.

Irritated with herself, she straightened up. It was idiotic to let Vanessa get to her like this.

'Mind you,' Vanessa continued maliciously, 'I suppose you'll be far too busy to go to London now that the new agency is opening up. I've told Adam that we must have this place revalued. We've really done everything with it that we can, and I rather fancy something a little larger. With this influx of people from London, we're bound to get a good price.'

She gave a complacent laugh which grated on Charlotte's ears, making her snap acidly, 'The increase in prices might be good news to you, Vanessa, but you seem to forget that, the moment prices start to increase, it means that young couples down at the bottom of the salary scale are priced out of the market and often forced to move away from an area where they might have lived all their lives. And it doesn't help when prices are driven up even further by greedy agents, who deliberately foster an upsurge in prices for their own benefit, without thinking about the unhappiness they're causing. If you really want my opinion, the kind of agent who cold-bloodedly opens up just to cash in on a boom area is quite despicable. They don't care about the misery they're going to cause to local people.'

'Well, of course *you're* bound to feel resentful,' Vanessa cooed, plainly delighted by Charlotte's outburst, and too late Charlotte realised her own stupidity.

It was too late to recall her words now, she realised, too late to do anything at all, as Vanessa suddenly smiled at someone over Charlotte's shoulder and said softly, 'Oliver...there you are. Come and meet Charlotte Spencer, although I'm afraid you won't get a very warm reception, and I must warn you that Charlotte has the reputation of being something of a man-hater.' Vanessa gave a light, tinkling laugh that grated on Charlotte's nerves. 'She's just been sounding off about the fact that you're opening up in competition to her. I don't think she's very pleased about it. But then I suppose that's understandable when you haven't been used to competition. Personally, I'm all for it.'

Charlotte struggled to control her anger and her chagrin. She wouldn't be in the least surprised if Vanessa had deliberately planned this, deliberately inveigled her into that outburst of righteous indignation so that she could make a fool of her, although honesty compelled Charlotte to admit that she had more than ably helped her. *Why* on earth hadn't she kept her thoughts to herself? *Why* allow Vanessa to provoke her? She felt humiliated and embarrassed, and was dreading turning round and facing 'Oliver', who, no matter what she might think of his business methods, deserved at least to be treated with the cordiality due to a newcomer to the area.

Gritting her teeth, she forced a smile to her mouth and turned round.

The stilted words of apology died on her lips as she found herself confronting the driver of the Jaguar car. Now close up, she saw that his eyes were even more astonishingly dark blue than she had thought, and that at close quarters his maleness was every bit as formidable as she had imagined.

Uncomfortably she felt heat flood her skin—the heat of embarrassment and confusion. It crawled painfully along her throat and burned her cheek-bones. She could almost feel Vanessa's gloating malice, as the blonde woman placed one dainty hand on the man's arm and smiled invitingly up at him.

'Never mind, Oliver,' Vanessa said softly. 'We aren't all as unfriendly as Charlotte. You mustn't mind her. She has a bit of a thing against men in general, I'm afraid. She's our local feminist.'

Charlotte was bitterly, achingly furious, but there was nothing she could do. She met the speculative glance he gave her full on.

She could imagine all too well what he was thinking: that her supposed feminist views were because she was not physically attractive enough to appeal to the majority of men. A man like him, so arrogantly self-assured of his masculinity, could never comprehend that there were women whose lives were perfectly happy without being built around some man.

As he extended his hand towards her, he said shockingly, 'I've been wanting to meet you.'

His words stunned her, holding her immobile. *Wanting* to meet her...? Why? Guiltily her mind

sped back to the afternoon, to her sneaky acqui-
sition of his parking spot.

'I'm afraid Charlie doesn't approve of you at all,'
Vanessa was saying bitchily. 'She seems to think
that just because you're successful you must be
guilty of sharp business practice.'

The blue eyes studied Charlotte rather too
shrewdly for her comfort for a moment, and then
he said smoothly, 'Well, naturally I'd deny such
an allegation, although speaking of sharp
practice——'

He was going to mention this afternoon, to amuse
himself at her expense by recounting what she had
done. Suddenly preternaturally sensitive, she felt
the stinging colour in her face deepen. He was
laughing at her, she knew. More amused than
angered by her supposed antipathy towards him,
enjoying her embarrassment.

Quite what would have happened if Adam had
not suddenly come up to tell Vanessa that the hired
staff were ready to serve dinner, Charlotte didn't
know.

As Vanessa, ignoring both Charlotte and Adam,
turned away, taking Oliver Tennant with her,
Charlotte discovered that she was trembling inwardly with a mixture of anger and impotence. Her
anger was caused as much by Oliver Tennant's pat-
ronising amusement at her expense as by Vanessa's
malice, and her frustrated impotence was the result
of her own inability to escape from the role
Vanessa had deliberately cast her into.

Vanessa had taken good care to paint her in
colours to Oliver Tennant which, while having a

basis in truth, were greatly exaggerated. Charlotte made no apology for her own belief that Oliver Tennant was cashing in on the property boom without any thought of how it would eventually affect their small community, but, given free choice, she would not have voiced those opinions so volubly or tactlessly in his presence. It was also true that there were certain aspects of the male sex which she personally found unappealing, but she was by no means the almost vigilante-like anti-men campaigner Vanessa had portrayed.

Unwittingly worrying at her bottom lip, as Adam escorted her through to the dining-room, Charlotte fumed over Vanessa's deliberately derogatory description of her as a feminist. Vanessa had used the word as a malicious insult. Charlotte resented being classified as a specific 'type' under any name; she was an individual, and, if her upbringing and physical attributes made it impossible for her to mimic Vanessa's cloying, clinging, supposedly 'feminine' manner with men, she preferred to think that it was because she had too much pride...too much self-awareness...too much self-respect to sink to Vanessa's level.

If the male sex couldn't *see* that beneath that sugary sweetness Vanessa was as corrosive as any acid, then they deserved everything they got.

Adam was saying something to her, clumsily trying to apologise, she recognised, her mood softening. Poor Adam. He most definitely did not deserve his atrocious wife. Sensing that he was genuinely concerned that she might be upset, she started to reassure him, and admitted, 'I did rather over-react. I didn't realise that the new estate agent was one of your guests.'

'Vanessa invited him. She met him when she approached him to ask him to value this place.' His face went dark red and he muttered uncomfortably, 'I don't know why she wants to move. I like this house...'

'It's all right, Adam,' Charlotte told him, wanting to comfort him. 'I've already recognised that most of the larger properties locally will probably go to the new agency. There's enough business here for both of us,' she added lightly, 'and by opening up I suspect that Oliver Tennant has saved me the necessity of taking on a partner.'

'He's got a very good reputation,' Adam told her earnestly, seizing her olive-branch. 'He started up originally in London and then expanded——'

'To take advantage of the current fashion for living in the country——' Charlotte finished for him a little grimly.

'Adam, where are you? I want you to sit here next to Felicity.' Vanessa's sharp voice broke into their conversation, as she gave Charlotte a false sweet smile and said nastily, 'Heavens, Charlie, you're not still boring on about poor Oliver, are you?'

Holding on to her temper, Charlotte forced herself to smile. She was bitterly regretting having ever accepted Vanessa's invitation.

Most of the other guests were people she knew, but not very well. They were incomers to the area in the main, like Vanessa and Adam, most of them pleasant professional couples in their mid-to-late thirties. All of them had bought their properties via her, and, although she believed that she had given them as professional and skilled service as they would get anywhere, she had no illusions. Were they to put their properties on the market tomorrow, it would be Oliver Tennant they instructed and not her.

Dinner was a long drawn-out affair of several minute courses. Toying with hers, Charlotte suddenly thought longingly of a bowl of home-made soup, the kind that Mrs Noakes from Little Dean Farm made, along with some of her home-made rolls, eaten across the well-scrubbed farm kitchen table, while a couple of early lambs bleated noisily in front of the Aga, and Holly, the Noakeses' now retired sheep-dog, lay across her feet.

She was not cut out for the sophisticated pleasures of life, Charlotte recognised broodingly. She had nothing in common with any of these people here, who all seemed to live frantically busy lives. The women's conversations were interspersed with references to the hopelessness of au pairs and the traumas of the pony club, the men's with mysterious references to 'insider dealing' and the horrors of London's traffic.

Moodily, Charlotte sipped spartanly at her wine. It was very rich and no doubt very expensive, but she wasn't enjoying it.

Smiling automatically at the man on her right at the circular table Vanessa favoured, as he described his battle with the local council to get planning permission for a conservatory large enough to house his new swimming-pool complex, for no reason she could analyse Charlotte was suddenly impelled to turn her head and look across the table.

To discover Oliver Tennant looking right back at her was so unnervingly disconcerting that she took a deep gulp of her wine and promptly choked on it, causing Vanessa to frown at her and her embarrassment to increase.

Why had he been looking at her like that? she wondered, when her embarrassment had eased. As though he had been studying her for quite some time; as though he knew every thought passing through her head; as though he almost felt sorry for her...sorry... Anger lashed at her, making her stiffen her spine and bare her teeth in a smile that made the man sitting next to her watch her nervously and wonder what on earth he had said. He was forty years old, and found modern women very confusing—this one more than most.

The meal seemed to drag on forever. Charlotte ached to be able to leave, but good manners forced her to stay, listening politely to the conversations going on around her, as they left the dining-room to finish the evening with coffee in the drawing-room.

Vanessa was discussing the summer fête, an annual late summer event of the village.

Deep in her own thoughts, Charlotte was stunned when Oliver Tennant got up and walked over to sit down beside her. The amused smile that briefly lightened his expression as he sat down puzzled her. She had no idea that it was the look of shock-cum-apprehension on her own face that had caused it.

Stiffly she made room for him beside her on the small pastel sofa.

'Vanessa tells me that you've only recently taken over your late father's agency,' he began questioningly.

Grimly aware of how Vanessa had probably run her down to him, Charlotte corrected coldly, 'Officially, yes, I took over on my father's death, but in fact I have been running the agency for nearly six years.' She turned her head so that she could look at him and added, 'But I should have thought you would have known this. Surely, when you plan to open up in a new area, you check up on the opposition first?'

'Yes, we do, but it was my partner who was responsible for this particular expansion. I've historically dealt with the London side of things, but earlier on this year we decided to split the partnership. He retained the country offices, while I retained the central London one... and this one.'

There was a look in his eyes that suggested to Charlotte that his split from his partner had not been overly amicable, and she wondered what had caused it.

'I had been intending to come and see you,' he was adding. 'While we are going to be in direct competition with one another, I thought——'

'What?' Charlotte challenged him bitterly. 'That we could form the sort of ring which antiques dealers are notorious for? I'm sorry, Mr Tennant,' she stood up abruptly, 'that isn't the way *I* do business. I don't believe in appealing to the more greedy side of people's natures. I prefer to set a realistic price on properties and not to encourage my clients to put outrageous prices on their homes. Nor do I believe in encouraging them to take on huge mortgages,' she added repressively. 'I don't believe that you and I could ever work harmoniously together.'

'Well, if we can't be friends...' he began musingly.

'We must be enemies. That suits me fine,' Charlotte told him grimly, and not entirely truthfully. There was something about him that warned her that he would be a formidable foe, but she had her principles and she did not intend to deviate from them. If that eventually meant that she lost so much business that her agency had to close, then so be it. She had her training to fall back on. She could always get a job in London, unappealing though that thought now was. She had her health, a very respectable bank balance, her own home...

Giving him a thin smile, she said curtly, 'I must be leaving. I'd better go and find Vanessa.'

'I'll come with you.'

She stared at him, and then flushed uncomfortably. For a moment she had thought he was suggesting that they leave together, when of course he had meant nothing of the sort. Angry with herself for the sudden and totally unexpected sensation churning her stomach, she turned away from him and looked for Vanessa.

Her hostess was plainly not particularly sorry to see her leave. Charlotte hated the insincere way Vanessa insisted on aiming a pouting kiss in the direction of her cheek.

Oliver Tennant was standing directly behind her, and when she stepped back to avoid Vanessa's embrace it was a shock to her senses to suddenly come up against the hard male warmth of him. She hadn't realised how close to her he was standing, and, when instinctively she tensed and turned to look over her shoulder, she was stunned to discover that only centimetres separated their faces. She could see the rough male texture of his skin, darkening already with the shadow of his beard. The eyes, which at a distance seemed uniformly dark blue, on closer inspection proved to have a lighter, almost metallic outer rim.

As she had stepped back, he had reached out automatically to steady her, and she was burningly conscious of the warm pressure of his hand on her arm, his fingers firm against her skin. She saw the way Vanessa focused on that point of contact between them, her mouth tightening, and wondered why on earth he hadn't simply stepped back from her.

'Oliver, surely *you're* not leaving? I wanted to have a word with you about putting this place on the market,' Vanessa pouted, darting a malicious glance at Charlotte.

'Another time, Vanessa, if you don't mind.'

He was still holding on to Charlotte's arm, and, as Vanessa started to say eagerly that perhaps he would like to call round in the morning, his grip relaxed slightly, and to Charlotte's shock his fingers moved almost absently against her skin, rather as though he were stroking the fur of a very ruffled cat, she recognised.

'Not tomorrow, I'm afraid. I'm still staying at the Bull at the moment, and I need to concentrate on finding myself some more permanent lodgings. However, I'll get my secretary to give you a ring.'

Charlotte could see that Vanessa was furious, but Oliver Tennant was either unaware of the other woman's feelings or indifferent to them, because he gave Vanessa a cordial smile and, without allowing Charlotte to say a word, almost guided her to the front door. And he had still not released her.

She waited until they were outside before pulling away from him and saying frigidly, 'Thank you, but *I* am capable of walking unaided.'

The smile he gave her made her heart somersault abruptly.

'I'm sorry about that, but it seemed a good way of escaping from Vanessa. It's always a problem, isn't it, when one has to deal with a client who is potentially looking for more than a purely business relationship? I expect it's something that's even harder for a woman to deal with than a man.'

Charlotte stared at him. There had been occasions when she had had to tactfully let the odd male client know that their relationship could only be based on business but, given Vanessa's cruel taunting of her lack of sexual appeal, she had hardly expected Oliver Tennant to assume that she would be the object of any man's desire, no matter how fleeting or implausible.

Neither had she expected him to make such a casual reference to Vanessa's rather obvious tactics to interest him in her sexually, and her mouth fell open a little as she contemplated this sudden and unexpected glimpse of a personality which seemed to be far more complex than she had initially assumed.

She had looked at him and dismissed him as a handsome, clever man more or less completely without principles or morals, used to trading on his sexual appeal when and where necessary, but he was making it plain to her that he did nothing of the sort.

Why? she wondered rawly. Was he doing it to get her off guard...to make her think that they were allies rather than enemies, and, if so, why? Did it amuse him perhaps to imagine that he could reduce her to the same competitive femininity he had so obviously aroused in Vanessa?

She remembered how Vanessa had described her as a man-hater, and wondered if he was one of those men to whom the challenge of sexual conquest mattered far more than any real emotional bonding with another human being. An inborn wariness warned her to tread carefully. He had released her now, and she moved away from him slowly. Every instinct she possessed warned her that it would be wise to keep this man at a distance. Already he had disturbed her far too much...made her aware of a certain illuminating lack in her life. Abruptly she turned round without answering him.

When she got in her car she was trembling inside. What was the matter with her? One look from an undeniably handsome and very male man and she was suddenly reduced to quivering awareness of her deepest feminine feelings. It was ridiculous. Even when she had been engaged, sexual desire had never strongly motivated her. In possible marriage to Gordon she had looked for companionship, children, shared interests and aims. She had never experienced that pulsing, urgent sensation of heat, coupled with an aching awareness of a deep inner emptiness that was afflicting her now.

It must be her age, she told herself briskly as she drove home. Nature's way of reminding her that she had still not fulfilled that most feminine biological drive: the need to create new life.

Yes, that was it, she decided, relaxing a little. She had always wanted children; her body had no awareness of the fact that her single status made such a situation impossible and, growing impatient with her refusal to listen to its urgings, it was stepping up its determination to remind her of what she was denying herself.

It was only later, when she was safely in bed, that she allowed herself to admit that the sensation that had pierced her had had nothing at all in common with the soft warmth that invaded her whenever she held a friend's baby, or played with a toddler. Determinedly she dismissed it. It had been a difficult day; her hormones were probably over-reacting in compensation. Tomorrow she would be able to laugh at herself for the way she was feeling right now.

CHAPTER THREE

CHARLOTTE was up early. She told herself that her restless night and inability to sleep had nothing whatsoever to do with the previous evening's disturbing run in with Oliver Tennant, but somehow or other her vigorous arguments remained unconvincing.

Perhaps it was the sharp spring sunshine pouring into the kitchen and highlighting the dinginess of the paintwork and units that was making her peer unusually closely into her most personal feelings and emotions as she was doing at her home, and with equally dissatisfying results, she admitted wryly.

The trouble was that, over the years of her father's illness, looking after him, running the business and trying to keep their often turbulent relationship on an even footing had left her with no time for soul-searching ... or redecorating.

She had never particularly thought of herself as the home-building type, and certainly she had no desire for a house which emulated the glossy magazine perfection of Adam's and Vanessa's.

But somewhere between the unwelcoming starkness of this house and the over-luxurious fussiness of Vanessa's there must be a happy medium.

Mrs Higham, who came in twice a week, kept the house reasonably clean, and every now and again when she could find the energy she herself spent the odd weekend thoroughly cleaning those rooms which were not in use. Mentally contrasting her large kitchen's lack of visual appeal and warmth with the comfortable cosiness of Sophy's tiny terraced-house kitchen, she acknowledged that something would have to be done.

Whether she stayed in the house or not, it was idiotic not to make any attempt to make it more welcoming. During her father's illness she had never had the time to spare for studying her surroundings with a critical eye, but now that she had . . . Yellow would be a good colour for this room, she decided musingly—a soft, sunny yellow to welcome the bright spring sunshine.

Another minute and she'd be rushing off to town to buy paint and brushes, Charlotte acknowledged ruefully. What was coming over her? She had never felt this almost nest-building urge to improve her home before. It must be the unexpected balminess of the spring sunshine, she told herself, firmly refusing to give in to her sudden desire to get to work on the kitchen almost immediately.

She had work to do. There would be time to spare for redecorating later in the year. If Oliver Tennant succeeded in taking her business away from her, she'd have plenty of time for playing with colour schemes and pots of paint.

When her father had originally opened his office in the local town, he had bought a small three-storeyed Tudor building, sandwiched in between its fellows down one of the old cobbled streets that ran off from the market square.

The site had advantages and disadvantages. The street had now been designated a conservation area, which gave it an appealing visual charm, an old-worldliness that suggested that within the building might be found the kind of thatched-roofed, rose-smothered country cottage of people's dreams. The street was also a draw to tourists and visitors who came to the town, which meant that there always seemed to be someone standing outside the old-fashioned mullioned windows staring in at the details of properties for sale. Against that, the cobbled street outside was now a pedestrian-only thoroughfare, with handsome black and gold painted bollards at either end of it to deter any driver tempted to use it as a short cut. This meant that any would-be clients had to make their way to the office on foot. In the past, when they had been the only estate agency in the area, this had not mattered, but now, with Oliver Tennant opening up...

His offices were on the outskirts of the town, not centrally placed like hers, but they were housed in the very large and popular shopping complex, purpose-built to accommodate the needs of the modern shopper and his or her car.

Charlotte was frowning as she parked her own car on the municipal car park on waste ground behind the Town Hall. Today was market day, which meant that the market square would be closed to parkers.

Sheila Walsh, who had been her father's secretary-cum-office-manager and who had been with them for ten years, welcomed her into the office above the reception area with a smile and a cup of coffee. Sheila was a married woman in her late forties with two grown-up children and a husband in the police force. She was a sensible, attractive woman to whom tact and discretion were second nature. Charlotte had found her help invaluable when she had first returned home to take up the reins of the business. *She* might have the qualifications, she had acknowledged, but Sheila had something far more valuable. She had experience and a way of dealing with people that Charlotte envied.

It had been at Charlotte's insistence that her father had agreed that Sheila should be promoted to 'office manager' and be given a salary and a percentage of their profits commensurate with the amount of work she did for them.

Without Sheila there was no way she could run the business as successfully as she did, Charlotte recognised, thanking her, and sitting down so that they could both go through the post.

'The new place opens up officially today,' Sheila commented. 'I wonder what he's like...the new man,' she mused.

Unwillingly Charlotte told her, 'I met him last night at Adam's and Vanessa's dinner party.'

It was part of Sheila's skill that she never probed. She waited now in silence, her eyebrows slightly raised.

She liked working with Charlotte. Initially, on hearing that her boss's daughter was coming home to take over the business, she had been uncertain as to whether or not she would stay on, but once she had realised how much Charlotte genuinely valued her, and how soft-hearted she really was beneath her rather austere exterior, she had put all her reservations to one side, and, as she told people quite genuinely now, her work brought her immense pleasure and satisfaction.

It saddened her that so many people misjudged Charlotte. Even her own husband had remarked, after first meeting her, that she was rather formidable. Sheila often wondered compassionately how it was that, while a woman could so easily see through another woman's armour to her vulnerability, a man was completely deceived by outward appearances and manners. Men were like children really, she often though scornfully; they always went for the gooey, heavily iced cake, not realising that once the icing was gone all they were going to be left with was stodgy and often unappetising sponge. Women were far more enterprising, far more aware; they knew that the very best things in life were often concealed by the most unappealing of exteriors.

Sheila Walsh was a traditionalist and made no apology for it. She loved her work and found it stimulating and rewarding, but it was her marriage and her family that formed the bedrock of her life. Without Rob to go home to at night, to talk over the events of the day with, to fight with and love, her life would be very arid.

Although Charlotte was older than her own daughter, Sheila acknowledged that she was inclined to feel a motherly protectiveness towards her. She was constantly urging her to buy new clothes, to go out and enjoy herself. Charlotte was such an attractive-looking girl in reality, but she tended to put men off with her brisk put-down manner. And yet one only had to see Charlotte with the children of her friends to realise what kind of woman hid behind her rather formidable exterior.

Sheila had got to know Charlotte very well over the last six years, and now, seeing the faint flush that stained her skin and the way she shifted her gaze, as though not wanting Sheila to look too penetratingly at her, Sheila became extremely curious about Oliver Tennant.

She had more intelligence than to ask too many questions, though, simply listening while Charlotte told her almost hesitantly about the dinner party.

'That Vanessa is an absolute bitch,' Sheila denounced roundly when Charlotte discovered that she had told her far more than she had intended to about her own chagrin and embarrassment during the evening. 'I can't see why men are too stupid to see through that kind of woman.'

'Sheila, do you get many male clients... well... making a pass at you?'

Sheila stared at her, not knowing what had motivated such a question. 'Some,' she acknowledged cautiously. 'Why?'

Charlotte wondered what Sheila would say if she told her that, far from making passes at her, the majority of men she showed round their properties seemed more intimidated by her than aroused.

'Oh... oh, it's nothing,' she fibbed, conscious of the uncomfortable colour suddenly staining her skin. Quickly changing the subject, she said more firmly, 'There's something I wanted to discuss with you this morning. Now might be a good time.'

Willingly Sheila agreed, listening intently while Charlotte outlined her thoughts on the possibility of their employing Sophy on a part-time basis.

'I haven't said anything to her as yet. I wanted to discuss it with you first. The burden of training her in the office routine would fall on you. I know at the moment we're busy enough to merit taking on extra staff. With summer round the corner, this is our busiest time of the year, but...'

Her frown betrayed what she was thinking, and Sheila finished quietly for her. 'With the new agency opening up, we're bound to lose some business and we may not be able to keep her on.'

'Mm... What do you think I should do?'

'I think you should speak to her, tell her what you've told me. In her shoes, I'd jump at the chance to get myself back into the swing of working. She'd just started training at the bank before she got married and had the twins, hadn't she? I'm not in favour of such young marriages... far too often girls get left on their own with young children to bring up and no proper financial or emotional support.'

'She is very short of money. The house is hers, but she's worried about how she's going to afford to keep it. I don't think she should sell. Not just now. It would mean going back to live with her parents.'

Sheila made a face. 'Her mother is a first-rate housewife, but she's more interested in keeping her home immaculate than she is in loving her grandchildren.'

'So you wouldn't object if I approached Sophy?'

Charlotte couldn't really understand why Sheila laughed and then hugged her.

It had come as a shock to her at first, this physical affection that Sheila showed to her. The death of her own mother when she was so young, her austere upbringing by her father, had meant that her life had been devoid of affectionate hugs and kisses. Often she wished she could be more like Sheila, who seemed to have no inhibitions about showing her feelings, no worries about having her overtures of friendliness and warmth rejected. The first time Sheila had hugged her like this, she had frozen as still as a statue. Now, with the ease of over five years of friendship between them, she was able to return her almost motherly embrace and say laughingly, 'I take it that means that you don't.'

'Look, why don't you go and see her now?' Sheila suggested. 'It's market day, and we'll probably have a fairly quiet morning. I can hold the fort here.'

'Strike while the iron's hot,' Charlotte said ruefully. She was halfway towards the door before she remembered something else. She stopped and turned to Sheila, asking impulsively, 'Sheila, do you by any chance know of a good local decorator? Oh, and someone who can build kitchen units?'

Stoutly concealing her surprise, Sheila considered and then told her, 'Yes, I think I do. I could have a couple of names and addresses for you when you came back, if you like. Are they for you, or...?'

'Yes. I was looking round the kitchen this morning. Whether I keep on the house or not, it needs some work doing on it. I suppose during Dad's illness I didn't have time to notice how dreary it is. I dare say the place hasn't been decorated since I was ten years old. It's clean and tidy enough, but . . .'

Sheila, who had visited the house on many occasions, tactfully said nothing. Privately she had always thought the house cold and unwelcoming, and she was only too pleased to see Charlotte doing something about improving her surroundings. She had brought up her own family on the maxim that a healthy desire to present an attractive appearance to the outside world showed self-respect and pride in one's own person.

The Volvo was reluctant to start again. Charlotte waited in exasperation for the petrol to stop flooding it before trying the ignition again. On the fourth attempt it started. She must do something about changing it, she told herself as she drove through the busy market-day streets, heading for the flat fen road that led to the small village where Sophy lived. The Volvo was proving irritatingly sluggish to drive, reminding her yet again that it was becoming increasingly unreliable.

As she drove through the flat fen countryside, she reflected that it was easy to tell which of the solitary substantial houses had been bought by newcomers and which had not. Those recently purchased had shiny coats of new paint, 'Victorian' conservatories, bright new cars in the drives. She was beginning to develop the long-time country livers' resistance to the influx of new blood, Charlotte thought wryly, and she tried to make

herself see the other side of the picture. Men like
Adam, for instance, who had brought new jobs to
the area; improved attendances at local schools;
improved facilities in the town.

Sophy lived in a small terraced cottage in a row
that fronted the village street. All of them had long
back gardens backing on to open fields, and,
although the houses were small, they sold quickly,
being snapped up by young couples looking for
their first home.

Charlotte parked her car outside and got out.

As she opened the gate, Sophy came to the front
door. The moment the twins saw Charlotte they tore
past their mother to fling themselves enthusiastically at her.

Sophy looked tired, Charlotte acknowledged,
studying the younger woman . . . too tired for a girl
of her age. She had lost weight, and her jeans hung
shapelessly on too thin hips. The twins, in contrast
to their mother, looked lively and happy, their
clothes clean and new.

Sophy adored her children and was a wonderful
mother, but the strain of constantly worrying about
money was beginning to tell on her, Charlotte
noticed, after Sophy had invited her inside and then
snapped sharply at her little boy as he started to
ask for a biscuit.

Guiltily she flushed, pushing her hair back out
of her eyes. 'I don't buy biscuits any more,' she
told Charlotte shakily. 'They're a luxury I can't
afford, but how can I make these two understand
that? They go round to Mrs Meachim's and she
gives them biscuits and orange juice, and then I

feel guilty because I can't do the same thing. I've even started to stop them going round so often. I don't want her to think——' She broke off helplessly. 'I'm glad you came to see me, Charlotte. I've definitely decided to put the house up for sale.' Her shoulders slumped defeatedly. 'The last thing I want to do is to move back in with Mum and Dad, but, no matter how carefully I try to budget, there just isn't enough money to feed and clothe the three of us and run the house. As it is, I'm having to buy the twins' clothes second-hand.' She made a face. 'I shouldn't complain really. With all the new money coming into the area, one of the mothers at the playschool has organised an unofficial clothes pool for mums who've got children's clothes that are too small but still have a lot of wear in them. I've got these two kitted out with the latest designer kids' wear for next to nothing, but just occasionally it would be nice for them to have something new.

'Katy came home from playschool crying the other day because one of the little girls had said she was wearing her dress.' She made another face. 'I know I can't afford to be overly proud...'

Charlotte, who had been trying not to show her pity while Sophy spoke, said quietly, 'Before you make a final decision about selling this place, I've got a proposition to put to you.'

'Work? For you?' Sophy exclaimed dazedly when Charlotte had finished. Already her shoulders seemed straighter. There was a pretty pink glow to her skin, and her eyes had brightened. Her face fell abruptly.

'But, Charlotte, I don't have any kind of experience in estate agency work.'

'I know that. Sheila is willing to train you up in the office routine, while I'll take you round with me, show you how to measure up et cetera. It will only be a part-time job at first,' she warned, 'and, to be honest with you, if Oliver Tennant is as successful as he intends to be I doubt that there'll be enough work for Sheila and me by the autumn, never mind for the three of us, but at least you'll have had a training, and who knows what might have happened by then?'

'I'll need to find a child-minder.'

'What about Mrs Meachim?' Charlotte suggested. 'I know she's not young, but as an ex-schoolteacher...'

'If she'd do it, there's no one I'd rather trust the kids with. She's marvellous with them.'

'I thought we could work out the hours to fit in around the twins.'

A faint shadow touched Sophy's face. 'You're not doing this just out of pity, are you?' she blurted out.

Charlotte shook her head firmly. 'No way. We *do* need the extra help, especially now with our busiest time coming up, and with new competition opening up we've got to be on our toes. We can't afford to keep people waiting.

'You'll want time to think it over,' she added considerately, but Sophy shook her head.

'No, I won't. It's a wonderful opportunity. I can't tell you how grateful I am. I'll have to check with Mrs Meachim that she'll have the twins, but subject to that . . . when do you want me to start?'

'Monday,' Charlotte suggested.

'Wonderful. Look, I'll give you a ring on Friday, if I may, just to let you know that I've got everything organised.'

As Charlotte got up to say her goodbyes to the twins, they both clung to her legs. Laughing, she picked the little girl up and carried her down the path with her. Sophy came with her carrying her son, but neither twin would let Charlotte open the gate and leave until they had had several hugs and kisses.

'I'm really grateful to you for giving me this job,' Sophy told her as she retrieved her children and Charlotte slipped through the gate.

'Don't be,' Charlotte told her firmly. 'I'm the one who's going to be grateful to you over the next few months.'

She was just about to move over to her car when a familiar dark blue Jaguar pulled up in front of her. Her heart started thumping as Oliver Tennant got out. How had he managed to track her down here? He must have either rung or been in to the office. What did he want?

He was coming towards her; she could feel the tension curling her stomach. He gave her a smile, and then to her shock turned aside to say easily to Sophy, 'Mrs Williams, I'm sorry to bother you, but I understand that you might be selling your house.'

Charlotte was stunned. She had heard of the keen business tactics of the more entrepreneurial of London's agents, but this! Her mouth dropped open, even her chagrin in realising that Oliver Tennant had not, as she had first supposed so stupidly, been looking for her forgotten as she fumed over his effrontery.

She could feel Sophy's surprise, and hear the awkwardness in her friend's voice as she said hesitantly, 'Well, no . . . I'm afraid I'm not.' She turned to Charlotte, looking for guidance.

Taking a deep breath, Charlotte said as calmly as she could, 'You go in, if you want to, Sophy. I'll deal with this.'

She could see Oliver Tennant frowning as Sophy scooped up her children and hurried indoors.

'I've heard of being quick off the mark,' she said bitterly, 'but this almost amounts to sharp practice. This isn't London, *Mr* Tennant. Out here we wait to be invited to act in a sale. We don't go out and chivvy our clients like salesmen.'

She was bitterly, furiously angry, and shockingly mingled with that anger was something almost close to pain . . . as though something inside her hurt at finding this incontrovertible evidence that Oliver Tennant was every bit as bad and unscrupulous in business as she had feared he would be. Pain . . . what a ridiculous idea. She ought to be feeling triumph, not pain.

'I could argue the point that sales people are exactly what we are,' Oliver told her, so obviously unperturbed that she was silenced. 'However, in this instance I'm afraid *you* have rather jumped to con-

clusions. I haven't come out here to persuade Mrs
Williams to give me her business. I simply want to
discuss with her the possibility of my buying her
house. I need somewhere to live…something short-
term and convenient while I look around for a more
suitable property. If all goes well down here I may
sell out the London end of the business and work
exclusively from here.'

If all goes well… If he managed to steal virtually all her business, he meant, Charlotte
acknowledged, hating him for putting her in the
wrong, and hating herself even more for making
such a fool of herself…

'I presume that that little bit of play-acting about
the house not being for sale was directed at me as
a fellow agent rather than as a prospective purchaser and, that being the case, I have no objection
to going through you. If I could make an
appointment to view…'

He was laughing at her, Charlotte was sure of it.
Well, she knew how to stop him doing so.

'Those might be *your* business methods, Mr
Tennant,' she told him crisply. 'They aren't mine.
The reason Sophy told you the house wasn't for
sale was quite simply because it isn't.'

'But I'd heard…' He was frowning now, looking
more irritated than remorseful.

'She *was* considering selling it…but…
circumstances have changed, and she's decided not
to.'

'So it looks as if we've both lost out,' Oliver told
her. 'Pity…I can't stay at the Bull forever, and

I'm not having any luck at all in finding rented accommodation.'

Charlotte bared her teeth at him and said saccharinely, 'Why don't you ask Vanessa to help you? She has at least three guest bedrooms empty... I'm sure she'd be delighted to offer you one.'

The look he gave her wasn't amused.

'I'm sure she would,' he agreed coolly.

He was blocking her path to her car, inadvertently she was sure, but suddenly, looking up at him—and she had quite a long way to look up, Charlotte realised warily—for the first time in her life she suddenly felt very, very vulnerable and fragile.

How ridiculous. He wasn't threatening her in any way. Any fool could see that he was a totally non-violent man, for all the powerful strength of his body. Whatever else she might consider him capable of doing, she couldn't deny that there was something about him that suggested he was the kind of man who would always be protective of those weaker than himself. There was almost a gentleness about him...

As she stared up at him, confused by her own feelings, by her awareness that in other circumstances this was a man she would very much have liked to have as a friend... or a lover... she felt her skin grow hot and, without thinking, heard herself saying breathlessly, 'I'm sorry if I misjudged your... your motives. I expect I did rather overreact, but things haven't been easy for Sophy. She was widowed some months ago. She desperately wants to keep her house and her independence. She was considering selling, but it wasn't something she wanted to do.'

She saw that he was frowning.

'I'm sorry to hear that. Is there no one who can help her...family?'

'She has parents, but——' Realising suddenly just how far she had dropped her guard, she said quickly, 'This is what happens, you see, when you get a property boom. Those at the lowest end of the market lose out. If Sophy sold her house, what chance would she have of ever rebuying, once the influx of London yuppies had pushed up local prices? Those with properties think only of the profit they're going to make. They don't think of the people who haven't yet got their feet on the first rung of the ladder...young couples, often with very low wages.'

'That isn't the fault of the agents,' Oliver told her quietly.

'No,' Charlotte agreed. 'It's the effect of market forces. We all know that, but you can't deny that there are unscrupulous, greedy agents.'

'Just as there are unscrupulous and greedy buyers and sellers,' Oliver agreed evenly, and then almost abruptly he added, 'Look, I know you don't like the fact that I'm opening up here, but I honestly believe that there is enough business for both of us. It isn't my intention to force your agency to close.'

His assumption that *should* it be his intention he *could* do so infuriated Charlotte, her anger overwhelming her earlier softening awareness of the man behind the image she had mentally created for him.

Not trusting herself to speak, she wheeled round sharply on her heel and unlocked her car door.

Mercifully this time it started at the first turn of the key, although Charlotte knew that her hands were shaking when she drove carefully away, her body intensely aware of the man standing on the pavement watching her, although she didn't betray by a single sideways glance her knowledge that he was there.

Why was this happening? she wondered miserably as she drove back to her office. She didn't want to feel like this about any man; she had got to an age where she had believed that she never would. She liked her placid, safe life; the fear of being hurt, of being found wanting, of being rejected had successfully protected her from the dangers of any potential involvement.

So why on earth now, when she should be safely past all this kind of nonsense, was she suffering these pangs of emotion and sensation, and for Oliver Tennant of all men?

It was a question she couldn't answer.

CHAPTER FOUR

'WELL, I think this shade would be perfect, especially with the wood you've chosen for the units.'

'Mm. I like this brighter yellow,' Sheila argued.

Sophy had started work with them on Monday morning, and now the three of them were sitting round the desk in the upper room studying paint-shade charts.

As good as her word, Sheila had produced the names and addresses of three painters and a couple of joiners. Choosing the wood for the kitchen units had been relatively easy. Charlotte had fallen immediately and heavily in love with the satin sheen of a pretty cherrywood, but choosing the paint for the walls was proving to be more of a problem.

Now, rather hesitantly, she produced a magazine and said quietly, 'I was wondering about *this* wall-paper... but I'm not sure.'

When she showed them the photograph the other two women instantly approved.

'It's perfect,' Sheila pronounced, 'and fun too. What is it?'

'It's Kaffe Fassett-style,' Charlotte told her. 'I've read about his work, and I saw this article mentioning the wallpapers he's designed. I thought this yellow one, with the pottery motifs.'

'It will be perfect,' Sophy agreed. 'And with some of those lovely old terracotta floor tiles. You've *got* to have an Aga, of course.'

Charlotte laughed. 'Well, as a matter of fact I *am* rather tempted. Vanessa has one, but she doesn't use it for cooking.'

Sheila clucked disapprovingly. 'What a waste. My mother had one years ago. She swore by it.'

'Well, most of the local farms still have them.'

'Have a dark green one,' Sophy suggested temptingly. 'It will look wonderful with your cherrywood.'

She had never realised that redecorating could be such fun, Charlotte admitted as she firm-mindedly tidied away her brochures and turned her attention to the post on her desk.

'Fun, yes, but expensive too,' Sheila said shrewdly, and then added, 'Has all this work you're having done mean you've decided to keep the house rather than sell it?'

Charlotte grimaced. 'I'd like to keep it. I think in the past it's been a case of the shoemaker's child going unshod as far as home has been concerned, and I hadn't honestly realised what potential the place had.' She wrinkled her nose and admitted, 'I think while Dad was alive I was too busy looking after him and running the business to notice our surroundings very much. Besides, he'd have had forty fits if I'd ever suggested changing anything. I thought when he died that the best thing I could do was to put the place on the market and have a fresh start somewhere else, somewhere that I felt was completely my own, but now...' She gave a faint sigh. 'I *am* tempted to keep it, but it's far too large for one person, and too expensive to run, especially if we lose a lot of business to Oliver Tennant.'

'Well, you know the answer to that one,' Sheila told her promptly, grinning as she exclaimed, 'You'll either have to get married or find yourself a lodger!'

She ducked as Charlotte threateningly threw a heavy brochure at her.

'Of the two,' Charlotte said loftily, 'I think your second suggestion was the more feasible.'

'Well, I should think seriously about it if I were you,' Sheila advised her. 'I must admit *I* wouldn't like living in that huge place all alone. It *is* rather remote.'

'It's two hundred yards off the main road,' Charlotte scoffed.

'Yes, down a narrow, rhododendron-lined drive that doesn't have any kind of lighting. Now that *is* something you should think about while you're having all this work done,' Sheila advised her firmly. 'If I were you, I'd see about getting some good security lights installed outside the house, and proper illuminations down the drive, plus a burglar alarm.'

'Heavens, the place will look like the Blackpool illuminations,' Charlotte complained, but Sophy shook her head.

'I agree with Sheila, you can't be too careful these days,' she said quietly. 'You read such dreadful things in the papers.'

For a moment all of them were quiet, soberly reflecting on the truth of what Sophy was saying, and then Charlotte said thoughtfully, 'Well, maybe I should make enquiries about having some kind of lighting on the drive.'

'And about looking round for a suitable tenant to share the running expenses of the house with you,' Sheila told her firmly.

'I'll think about it,' Charlotte promised, having no intention of doing any such thing. She liked her privacy too much, for one thing, and for another... Well, much as she liked Sheila, she had to acknowledge that the older woman had a decided tendency towards matchmaking. She was pretty sure that the kind of tenant Sheila had in mind for her would be male, and eligible.

'I drove past the new agency's offices this morning,' Sheila informed her, changing the subject. 'Very glitzy and modern, but I felt that it was a little too streamlined, if you know what I mean. It might appeal to the local high-fliers, but I think the older people would find it rather intimidating. I didn't see the new man there, though.'

'I've seen him,' Sophy told her, before Charlotte could speak. She grinned enthusiastically. 'He's a real hunk.' She laughed at the disgusted sound Charlotte made in her throat and insisted, 'Well, he is. He seemed nice too... as though he knew exactly how women were going to react to him.'

Charlotte snorted again and muttered under her breath.

'Vain.'

'No, that wasn't what I meant,' Sophy complained. 'It was almost as though he was asking you to look beyond his looks. I can't explain properly what I mean. It's just that he made me think that he was basically nice.'

'Nice?' Charlotte protested. 'Of course he wants you to think he's nice. That's all part of the act he uses to secure business.'

But, even as she spoke, she knew she wasn't being entirely fair. Like Sophy, she had been struck by an essential lack of vanity and conceit in Oliver Tennant.

Despite Vanessa's attempts to depict her as some kind of man-hating anti-male campaigner, he had treated her with the same degree of politeness he had shown to Sophy. At first glance he had seemed so essentially male that she had expected him to respond immediately to Vanessa's derogatory comments about her, by challenging her in some way, or trying to make her look even more stupid than Vanessa had done, but instead he had ignored it...had looked at her in a way which had suggested that he preferred to make his own judgements rather than to rely on those of other people. A tiny wistful thought crept into her mind...an odd weakening sensation that made her wonder how he would have reacted to her had she been sexually desirable.

Immediately she clamped down on the thought, horrified that it should have formed at all. So powerful was her sense of anger against herself that her skin lost colour, causing Sheila to frown and ask quietly, 'Charlotte, are you all right? You've gone quite pale.'

Privately Sheila thought that, after the trauma of her father's death, and the strain of nursing him for so long plus running the business, it was a wonder that Charlotte hadn't cracked up completely.

If it weren't for the opening of this new agency, she would have been urging Charlotte to take a proper holiday—something she hadn't done since she returned home. Much as she herself had liked Henry, there was no doubt that he had been something of a tyrant, and privately she considered that he had never valued Charlotte as he ought.

She was well aware of Charlotte's lack of confidence in herself as a woman, and longed to tell her that, if only she could learn to project an image of sexual confidence, she would soon discover how very attractive the opposite sex could find her, but for all her independence Charlotte had a very vulnerable side to her nature, and Sheila knew she would hate her mentioning a subject she thought completely hidden from anyone else.

She was such an attractive young woman, and many many times Sheila had longed to shake Henry for the damage he had done to his daughter's personality with his constant put-downs. The trouble with Henry had been that he was one of the old-fashioned chauvinists who could never accept a daughter in place of a son.

Over the years Sheila had done her best to introduce Charlotte to a variety of young men, but invariably she would clam up with them, holding them so stiffly and determinedly at a distance that Sheila had shaken her head in despair.

Now, as she opened the post alongside Charlotte, she glanced idly out of the window and then whistled softly under her breath.

'What's wrong?' Charlotte asked, without lifting her head, absorbed in the letter she was reading.

'It looks as if we've got our first client of the week...and what a client!'

The awe in Sheila's voice was enough to make Charlotte put down the letter she was studying and walk across the room, to stand behind Sheila looking curiously through the window.

She saw him immediately, and, as though by some machiavellian instinct, he paused and stood still looking directly at her, so that she had no opportunity to move out of his view.

She felt like a schoolgirl caught ogling him, and her face burned dark red.

'What's wrong?' Sheila asked her.

'That's Oliver Tennant,' she told her friend tensely.

'Ah.'

The short word held a wealth of expression.

'I wonder why he's coming here,' Sophy murmured.

'There's only one way to find out,' Charlotte told them briskly. 'Sheila, you'd better go down and find out. Sophy, perhaps you should go with Sheila and get some experience of dealing with the public.'

She saw the look her two companions exchanged, but pretended not to. There was no way she was going to go down to the reception desk and face him—not after she had seen the slow, almost

boyish smile which had curved his mouth when he'd
looked up and found her watching him.

It was a very dangerous thing, that smile, in-
viting her to share in some special secret kind of
magic, when in reality he had been laughing at her.
A very deceptive smile. A very deceptive man, she
reminded herself, grimly forcing her attention back
to her post.

When ten minutes had passed without Sheila's
and Sophy's returning she began to feel distinctly
twitchy. She imagined him walking round their
downstairs office, studying the brochures on
display, reading the details which she herself wrote,
meticulously trying to show each property to its advantage, without any embroidery that might lead a
prospective purchaser to claim that they had been
misled.

Where a property had a fault, she always made
a point of listing it on the final page of her brochures, where she always placed the property's good
and bad points under the headings 'Advantages'
and 'Disadvantages'. To be fair, which she always
was, one man's flaws were another's attractions.

A house served not by mains drainage but by
septic tank would be anathema to some, while
others would consider this to be no problem at all.
For purchasers with children, proximity to schools
must come higher on their list of priorities than,
say, being within walking distance of village shops,
which might be a prime requirement of an older
couple.

Remembering her own working life in London,
Charlotte was well aware that this was not normal

city practice, where competition forced agents to be far more ruthless, far more elastic with the truth.

She abhorred that kind of selling, and dreaded discovering that Oliver Tennant intended to introduce it into their quiet country life, thus forcing her to either yield the major share of the market to him, or compete with him on the same footing.

Nervously she looked at her watch. There was no sign of him leaving. What on earth was he doing? Curious though she was, she was not going to give in to the temptation to go downstairs and find out.

In the end it was twenty minutes before she saw him striding back across the street in the direction he had come. Maddeningly, before Sheila and Sophy could report back to her, there was a small flurry of business, and it was almost half an hour after he had left before Sheila came back upstairs to tell her breathlessly and triumphantly, 'You'll never guess what ... I've found you your lodger!'

As she stared at Sheila in silence, a horrid suspicion struck Charlotte.

'Not ... not Oliver Tennant,' she protested in dismay.

'The very same,' Sheila told her cheerfully, apparently oblivious to the fact that, far from sharing her delight in the news, Charlotte was looking decidedly unhappy.

'Don't worry,' Sheila added. 'I've warned him about the alterations et cetera and he says they won't bother him. Apparently he eats out a good deal. In fact, he says you'll hardly see him. He came in looking for a small property to rent, but I explained how seldom we get rented stuff, especially

in the tourist season when everyone with a spare
room to let is looking to make a bit extra from B
and B.

'He was just about to leave when I remembered
what we'd been saying earlier, so I told him about
your place. I explained all the disadvantages, don't
worry,' Sheila went on, before Charlotte could in-
terrupt and inform her that it wasn't Oliver
Tennant's reaction to the disadvantages of becoming her lodger that worried her, but the fact
that Sheila had actually made such a suggestion in
the first place.

'As a lodger he'll be ideal,' Sheila enthused. 'He's
prepared to pay well above the norm. He did ask
if it would be possible for him to have the use of
a room to work in, and I immediately thought of
your dad's old rooms. Remember when he was first
ill, how he insisted on trying to work at home, and
we kitted out the adjoining bedroom with a desk
for him?'

Charlotte's hissed indrawn breath must have
registered what she was feeling, although Sheila
misinterpreted the reason for it, as she turned to
her and said gently, 'Yes, I know how you must
feel, but your dad's gone, Charlotte. I'll bet you
haven't even been in those rooms since he died. I
know when I lost my mother I couldn't bring myself
to go near her bedroom for months, but once I
did... Well, once I'd sorted through her things and
turned the room back into a guest room, I felt as
though I'd finally come to terms with her death. I
know it will be difficult for you having someone
else in those rooms——'

'Difficult?' Charlotte exploded, unable to keep back what she was feeling any longer. 'Sheila, you *can't* seriously stand there and tell me that you've really invited Oliver Tennant...to become my lodger. Please tell me it's just a joke,' she implored grimly.

Sheila stared at her. 'But I thought you'd be pleased.'

'Pleased? *Pleased!*' Charlotte was stunned. 'How *could* you think that?'

'Well, for one thing, it will give you an opportunity to keep an eye on him, so to speak,' Sheila told her. 'And for another...well, you couldn't really find a more suitable lodger, could you?'

'But, Sheila, I don't *want* a lodger.'

Now it was Sheila's turn to stare. 'But only this morning you said——'

'No,' Charlotte corrected her ruthlessly. '*You* said. To be quite honest with you, I think I'd rather sell than share my home with Oliver Tennant—not that it's come to that yet. You'll have to telephone him and tell him that there's been a mistake.'

She looked away from Sheila as she spoke, cravenly hoping that her friend wouldn't see the emotions she was trying to hide.

Oliver Tennant...sharing her home. Her heart was still thudding like a sledgehammer, the shock of Sheila's announcement reverberating through her body. She tried in vain to picture the two of them sharing the old house in cosy intimacy, but her mind refused to conjure up any such visions. Oliver Tennant might just be desperate enough to believe that the two of them could live alongside one another in harmony, but she couldn't believe it. And besides, what on earth would people say? She closed her eyes in stunned dismay that Sheila, of all people, could actually have suggested that Oliver Tennant lodge with her.

Almost as though she had read her mind, Sheila said cautiously, 'I suppose you're worried about what people will think.'

'That's certainly one of my worries,' Charlotte agreed grimly. 'Honestly, Sheila, you know what people are like round here.'

'Well, yes, but look at it this way—with both of you being unattached, people were bound to gossip, to speculate, to connect the two of you together. This way, the whole thing will be a nine-day wonder and then forgotten.'

Charlotte raised her eyes heavenwards and denounced, 'I can't follow your logic at all. You'll have to ring him.'

As she turned her back, Sheila and Sophy exchanged glances. Clearing her throat, Sophy said quietly, 'It's no business of mine, I know, but I think Sheila did the right thing. People round here love a bit of intrigue and mystery; if they think that you and Oliver Tennant are going to become deadly enemies fighting for the major share of the local property market, you'll both become subject to all kinds of speculation. This way, people will just assume that you've come to some harmonious agreement. The fact that he's sharing your home will raise a few eyebrows at first, but once people realise——'

'How unlikely that a man like him would be interested in someone like me,' Charlotte supplied bitterly for her. 'Yes, well, I suppose you're right about that, but neither of you seem to have stopped to think that I might not want a lodger at all ... any lodger.'

'But you agreed earlier that it would be a good thing. Personally I'll feel a lot easier in my mind if he is there. I've been worrying about you ever since Henry died and I don't mind admitting it. You are off the beaten track, you know, no matter how much you might deny it,' insisted Sheila.

Biting back the acid comment that a bedridden father would surely have been no defence against any would-be attacker, Charlotte struggled to preserve her temper. She couldn't understand what had got into Sheila. She was normally so circumspect...

'I can't understand why Oliver Tennant should have agreed with your suggestion.'

'Agreed? He nearly bit my hand off,' Sheila told her, with what Charlotte suspected was an exaggeration. 'I only mentioned it idly really, as you do, but he insisted that I tell him more about the house and the more I told him, the more he seemed to like the idea.'

'*He* might, but *I* don't!' Charlotte retorted.

'Well, he's going to see about getting a tenancy agreement drawn up,' Sheila continued. 'It seems that, because they deal with rented property such a lot in London, he knows a solicitor who's familiar with the ins and outs of such agreements. He said he'd call round with it tomorrow.'

Charlotte stared at her. She couldn't believe what was happening.

'Look, why don't you sleep on it before making any decision?' Sheila counselled. 'He struck me as being very pleasant ... and very trustworthy.'

'Well, I'm certainly not worried that he's going to be driven mad with lust for me,' Charlotte told her forthrightly, making Sophy giggle.

'Well, what *are* you worried about, then?' Sheila asked her.

For someone who was normally so astute, Sheila was being remarkably obtuse. Surely it was obvious why Charlotte didn't want the man living with her? He was her competitor, for one thing, and for another ... well, for another ... Well, she just would not feel comfortable about sharing her home with such a very male man, but somehow she couldn't bring herself to voice these feelings to her friends.

'Look, think it over, and if you still feel tomorrow that you don't want him as a lodger then I promise I'll tell him,' Sheila suggested.

'Very magnanimous of you,' was Charlotte's sour response. She'd no intention of changing her mind, no matter what Sheila might think, and she'd have preferred her friend to telephone Oliver Tennant and tell him her decision right away, but Sheila was behaving as though the matter was settled, leaving her little option but to grudgingly accept her suggestion or telephone him herself.

She wasn't sure why she should feel it was impossible for her to do that; she only knew that it was.

For the rest of the day she could not concentrate properly on what she was doing. Leaving Sophy in Sheila's charge, she went off to value a pair of semi-detached cottages belonging to a local farm. With so much mechanisation and less need for agricultural workers, the cottages had been empty for some time. Now the farmer wanted to sell them.

They were in a very dilapidated state, nearly a mile off the main road, with no gas and no mains drainage. With planning consent to turn them into one larger house, and an offer from the farmer to supply some land with them, they might just appeal to someone with enough money and enthusiasm to take on the job of remodelling them, but Charlotte doubted that she would be able to sell them as two separate homes.

The farmer proved surly when informed of her misgivings. Typically, he wanted to achieve the most money for the least output, and Charlotte wasn't surprised when he told her that he was going to try 'yon new agent', adding insultingly, 'Women...they don't understand nothing about business.'

Charlotte was furious, but hid her anger, saying smoothly that of course it was his decision. She couldn't regret losing the sale—the farmer would have been an awkward client to deal with—but she couldn't help acknowledging that without Oliver Tennant to turn to the farmer might have been more disposed to consider her suggestions.

Well, good luck to him, and good luck to Oliver Tennant if he told the farmer that he would be able to secure sales as two separate houses. She didn't

envy him that task, she thought sourly, and yet the
farmer's parting insult about her sex rankled, and
for some reason as she drove home it was Oliver
Tennant who was the object of her acid thoughts
of the male sex and its arrogance, rather than the
farmer who had made the comment.

The Volvo was still playing up, and on impulse,
instead of returning to the office, she drove to the
local country town some twenty miles away where
she knew there were several reputable dealers.

She wasn't sure just what sort of car she should
get—something reliable . . . another Volvo perhaps,
but a smaller model.

The salesman proved to be very informative and
helpful. When she left the showrooms half an hour
later, she had several brochures and a fairly clear
idea of what she was going to buy.

On the way home she had to pass another car
showroom. This one had several immaculate
gleaming Jaguar saloons in its window. She sighed
a little enviously, looking at them. The Oliver
Tennants of this world might be able to afford such
unashamed luxury, but she could not.

He must be desperate indeed for somewhere to
live if he was prepared to consider lodging with her,
but then, she reflected contemptuously, he probably
considered that she would make a far better
landlady than someone like Vanessa, whose ego
would constantly need massaging, and who would
expect far more from him than the simple payment
of a set sum of money each month. It would be
obvious to him that a woman like herself would

never dare to imagine that a man like him would consider her in any remote way desirable.

Sheila would describe him rather old-fashionedly as 'eligible'. Charlotte knew that he wasn't married, but he was a man in his mid-thirties, who must surely have had at least one long-standing relationship, and perhaps more. She wondered if there was anyone special in his life right now, and then caught herself up. What possible concern could that be of hers?

Frowning fiercely, she forced herself to confront what was in her mind. All right, so he was a very attractive man, a man to whom she seemed to be far from as immune as she should be, but the matter started and ended right there. She had long ago learned the folly of dreaming impossible dreams, and anyway she was far too sensible these days to imagine that loving someone and being loved by them was enough to guarantee perfect happiness.

Marriage, especially these days, was something that required hard work and complete commitment from both parties. When she had finally abandoned any idea of marrying, she had consoled herself with the knowledge that even the best relationships of her friends were sometimes fraught and difficult. If she did not have the closeness that came from sharing her life with a partner, then neither did she have the trauma and pain that such closeness inevitably brought.

When she eventually left the office an hour after Sheila and Sophy had gone home, it had started to rain. The house, when she turned into the drive, seemed to lift an unprepossessing and austere outline towards the sky. The rhododendron-lined drive, pitted with holes in places, suddenly seemed forbidding and almost frightening. Until this morning, she had never even thought about the house's remoteness, nor the fact that the drive so effectively sheltered it off the road, but this evening for some reason she was acutely conscious of the silence around her—conscious of it and vaguely alarmed by it.

Once she had stopped the car, she didn't linger, but instead hurried to the back door, suddenly anxious to get inside the house. When she was in, although it was something she rarely did, she found herself slipping on the security chain as she closed the door.

Heavens, she wasn't going to turn into one of those timid types expecting the worst to happen at every corner, was she?

While she waited for the coffee to filter, she played back the messages on her answering machine.

The joiner had telephoned to say that he was able to start the kitchen sooner than planned, and there was a message from the decorator Sheila had recommended. She would phone him later and ask if he could obtain the wallpaper she liked.

As she drank her coffee and ate her evening meal, she found herself wondering what Oliver Tennant would think of her new kitchen. Would he find her choice of décor overly feminine or...?

Abruptly she put down her coffee-mug, revolted by her own weakness. It didn't matter what the man thought. For one thing, he wasn't going to get an opportunity to voice his thoughts, because first thing tomorrow morning she was going to make Sheila telephone him and retract that idiotic suggestion that he become her lodger.

After she had finished her meal, she stared disconsolately out into the rainswept garden. She had planned to do some work in it this evening. Whenever she felt on edge or bad-tempered she found an hour or so spent pulling up weeds excellent therapy. Tonight she was denied that release, and instead she wandered aimlessly around the house.

It was a family home really, with its large high-ceilinged rooms and its funny little passages...a house that should be filled with noise and laughter.

When she walked into the drawing-room that was never used, she sniffed the stale air with distaste and went to open the french windows.

The fresh, clean scent of the rain filled her nostrils as she eyed the dull beige walls and carpet with distaste. Why had she never noticed before how hideous this room was? She looked up at the ceiling, trying to imagine the plasterwork picked out in different colours, and then studying the rather attractive period fireplace. This room faced south, and she tried to imagine it decorated in shades of soft yellows and blues...

Restlessly she left the drawing-room and walked round the house, ending up outside the door to her father's old suite of rooms. Beyond the door lay the room her father had used as his study-cum-sitting-room at the start of his illness, his bedroom and his bathroom.

Since his death she hadn't been inside them. The vicar's wife had arranged for his clothes and personal effects to be removed, and Mrs Higham had gone through the rooms giving them a thorough clean. Now, with her hand on the door, Charlotte felt a deep shudder of pain go through her.

Their relationship should have been so different, she acknowledged. She had loved her father, but had never been able to express that love because she had always known that she was not the son he had wanted. On the surface they had got on well enough, but under that surface there had been a distance between them, a lack of closeness which had hurt her deeply when she was child, but as she had grown up she had learned to accept it, just as she had learned to accept that in her father's eyes she would never be what he wanted.

Was that why she had always felt so inferior and vulnerable with other men—because she expected them to reflect her father's disappointment in her?

It was a disturbing thought, and one she did not want to pursue. It was too late to go back now, looking for motives, for reasons to explain away her lack of appeal for the male sex. She had long ago come to accept that she was the way she was. Too late now to look back and wonder if perhaps things could have been different.

Gordon had after all laid it on the line for her when they had broken their engagement. He did not find her desirable, he had told her; he liked her as a person, but as a woman... Those words were still buried inside her, sharp slivers of steel that still ached and hurt, that had left a wound long after she had got over the loss of Gordon himself.

When she finally steeled herself to walk into her father's rooms she was disconcerted by her lack of emotional reaction. They were simply rooms, furnished with heavy but good furniture, their décor dull and uninspiring, although her father's desk and the comfortable armchair behind it gave one room a certain austere masculinity.

She tried to picture Oliver Tennant sitting behind that desk, holding her breath tensely, relieved when she found it impossible to conjure up his image and superimpose it on to her father's chair. In the morning she would insist on Sheila's telephoning him and telling him that it was impossible for him to lodge with her.

Her mind firmly made up, she went back downstairs. She had some paperwork to do, which would fill her time far more profitably than mooching about the house the way she was doing at the moment.

CHAPTER FIVE

THE next morning the Volvo refused to start once again. This time Charlotte had to call out the local garage, and only arrived at the office after the mechanic had spent over half an hour coaxing the reluctant engine to fire.

In consequence she was both out of temper and out of patience when she eventually hurried across the square and opened the office door, and the last person she wanted to see standing there, somehow looking far taller than she remembered, was Oliver Tennant.

He had his back towards her as he studied their property brochure displays, but as she walked in he swung round, his eyes crinkling a smile that made her stomach somersault dangerously.

'Mr Tennant.' She said his name in as crisply professional a manner as she could. He was holding an envelope in his hand and her heart sank. This must be the tenancy agreement. He hadn't wasted any time, but, in all fairness to him, she had to acknowledge that the chance of his finding somewhere else to rent at this time of the year was very small.

'Miss Spencer,' he acknowledged formally, and then frowned, asking far more personally, 'Is everything all right?'

Charlotte stared at him, conscious of the fact that Sheila was watching them both.

'Yes, of course it is. Why shouldn't it be?' she demanded aggressively, and was stunned as he casually stretched out one hand and brushed his fingers over her cheekbone in something that was so like a caress that she drew in her breath, shocked by the sensations evoked by his touch.

Her eyes must have registered her feelings because for a breathless second his own darkened, and then he said evenly, 'You've got oil on your face. I wondered if your car had broken down.'

Oil on her face. Damn that mechanic. No wonder he'd been grinning when he drove away. Why hadn't he *said* something? Charlotte fumed, resisting the impulse to rush to the nearest mirror and see how much of an idiot she looked.

'It's got a starting problem,' she admitted through gritted teeth.

Behind her she heard the door open as someone came in, but before she could turn round Oliver Tennant was saying easily, 'Well, perhaps, once I've moved into your place, I can repay your kindness by giving you a lift into town...at least until you've got your car fixed.'

Charlotte was furious; she opened her mouth to disabuse him of his idea that he would be 'moving in', as he termed it, but before she could say a word a familiar and decidedly shrill female voice cut in acidly.

'You're moving in with Charlotte, Oliver? Good heavens...why?'

Vanessa! Charlotte closed her eyes on a wave of disbelief. Of all people to have overheard Oliver's comment, Vanessa was the very last one she would have chosen.

'Charlotte has kindly offered to take me on as a lodger until I find a house of my own,' she heard Oliver say smoothly to Vanessa.

'But why? I told you *we* have a spare room. Heavens, Oliver, what can you be thinking of? Have you *seen* Charlie's house? You'll be very uncomfortable there.'

As Charlotte turned round, Vanessa said aggressively to her, 'You can't possibly be serious about this, Charlotte. I mean, think of what people will say. An unmarried woman...an unmarried man...living together.' She gave an acid laugh. 'Of course, I don't suppose for a moment that anyone will believe Oliver is interested in you, *his* reputation will be safe enough, but people are bound to wonder about you...to speculate. You'll be in a very vulnerable position, a woman of your age.'

Charlotte wasn't sure what prompted the blinding anger that overwhelmed her, or what hurt her the most. Vanessa's insinuation that Oliver couldn't possibly be interested in her only underlined her own views, after all...perhaps it was the fact that she was voicing it, and so cuttingly, in front of Oliver himself. An Oliver who was oddly silent.

Carried along on a powerful surge of anger, Charlotte heard herself saying acidly, 'I'm sure you're exaggerating, Vanessa, and that no one will give the fact that Oliver is lodging with me a second thought. At least, no one with any common sense.

It seems a very sensible arrangement to me. Oliver needs a place to live, and to be quite frank I could do with some temporary help with the running expenses of the house while I decide whether to keep it or sell it.'

'*Keep it?* It's a family house,' Vanessa told her shortly. 'What on earth would you do with it? After all, it's not as though you're likely to marry... not at your age.'

Seething with anger, Charlotte turned away from her, and was then shocked into immobility as unbelievably she heard Oliver saying coolly, 'You're rather behind the times, you know, Vanessa. In London very few women contemplate marriage these days until they're well established in their careers and into their early thirties. The days when a woman's sole aim in life was to secure a husband are long gone. It's we men these days who are having to do the chasing and persuading.'

Vanessa stared at him, obviously taken aback by his criticism, and then rallied to say coquettishly, 'Oh, come on, Oliver, don't try to tell me that *you've* ever had to chase any woman.'

He had rescued her, Charlotte recognised in surprise. He had quite deliberately stepped in and rescued her from Vanessa's malice.

His behaviour confused her, and left her feeling even more vulnerable and unsure of herself. Why had he done it? Because he felt sorry for her? Because it was in his own interests in view of the fact that he wanted to lodge with her? Or because he had genuinely believed what he had said?

Angry with herself for letting her thoughts wander, she said curtly to Vanessa, 'What exactly did you want, Vanessa?'

'Oh, I saw that Oliver was here and I came in to remind him that he promised to come round and value our house,' Vanessa told her carelessly.

Stunned by her rudeness, Charlotte swallowed her anger and said as pleasantly as she could, 'Well, as the two of you obviously have business to discuss, I'll leave you to it.'

However, as she turned to walk away, Oliver stopped her. The sensation of his hand resting lightly on her arm was like a small electric shock. As she reacted automatically to it, her eyes widening as she turned towards him, he said evenly, 'This is neither the time nor the place for such a discussion, Vanessa. If you'd care to ring me at *my* office...' And then, giving her a dismissive nod, he said to Charlotte, 'I've brought a copy of the prospective tenancy agreement round for you to look at. You'll want your solicitor to go over it, of course, but if you could spare me five minutes to discuss it with you...'

Over his shoulder Charlotte watched as Vanessa gaped at his back like a stranded fish. She would not have been human if she hadn't relished Vanessa's discomfort a little, she told herself as she saw the hard, angry colour darken the other woman's face, suddenly making her look far less attractive and much, much older.

However, it was only after the door had slammed after Vanessa that she realised too late that she had virtually committed herself to agreeing to Oliver

Tennant's becoming her lodger. She opened her mouth to tell him that there had been a misunderstanding and that there was no way she was going to allow him to set a single foot inside her home, when she suddenly realised that, if she did so, Vanessa would undoubtedly assume that she had changed her mind because of what *she* had said.

The thought of anyone thinking that she placed the slightest bit of importance on Vanessa's ridiculous suggestions about her reputation was so revolting that the words of denial remained locked in her throat.

Somehow or other, she found herself upstairs in the office, with Oliver standing beside her desk while she read quickly through the document he had given her.

It seemed simple and straightforward enough. A month's notice on either side of any termination of their agreement which was to run for a period of six months and thereafter to be renewed, subject to mutual consent.

The rent Oliver was prepared to pay was more than generous, and as she read the document he was saying something about making sure that he did not impinge on her privacy.

'Sheila has explained to me about your kitchen alterations. I'll be eating out most of the time anyway. Between us we can organise things so that there's no conflict...no invasion of one another's privacy.'

He was so rational about everything, so organised, that she couldn't find the words to object to what he was saying to her. Somehow or other, when he left the office half an hour later, it seemed that willingly or not she was going to have him as a lodger.

'I told you he was nice,' Sheila said approvingly when he had gone. 'I loved the way he defended you to Vanessa. My goodness, the look on her face,' she chuckled, until Charlotte said sharply,

'I'm not a child, Sheila. I could quite easily have defended myself.'

Listening to Sophy and Sheila congratulating her on finding such a perfect tenant, gritting her teeth while Sheila said triumphantly, 'I'll feel so much better now, knowing that there's a man living there again,' Charlotte wondered why it was that everyone seemed so oblivious to the fact that she was far from delighted by the way things had turned out.

It was her own fault, though. She had had her chance. She could have said in front of Vanessa that the latter was quite right and that it was completely impossible for Oliver to lodge with her...so why hadn't she done so?

Because she hadn't been able to endure Vanessa's triumph if she did. So now she was paying for her moment of pride and rebellion with an unwanted lodger. She had no one to blame but herself.

Now, of course, she would have arrangements to make, and Mrs Higham would have to be informed. Heaven alone knew what she would think of Oliver's residence at the house.

Behind her, Sheila and Sophy were chuckling over the way Oliver had so successfully routed Vanessa. Charlotte listened absently to them, gnawing worriedly at her bottom lip. What on earth had she done? She couldn't share her home with Oliver Tennant, of all men.

Why not? an inner voice demanded acidly. Do you really have so little faith in your own self-respect? Do you honestly believe that, just because you'll be living under the same roof, you're likely to do something stupid like...?

Like what? she asked herself bitterly. Like falling in love with him? Of course she wasn't; she was far too sensible for such folly.

Gordon had described her personality very accurately when they had broken their engagement.

'You're so sensible, Charlie,' he had complained. 'You always do the right thing.'

Even though their engagement had ended by mutual consent, even though she had acknowledged a thousand times since then her relief at not finding herself trapped in a marriage she realised now would never have worked, there was still a small raw place inside her that hurt from time to time, and which was hurting now.

Would Sheila be encouraging her so warmly to take Oliver Tennant as a lodger if she were a different type of woman, an attractive, sensual woman to whom Oliver Tennant was likely to be drawn as a man?

No, Sheila had no qualms about foisting Oliver off on her because she knew quite well that any relationship which developed between them was bound to be free of any sexual connotations, on Oliver's part at least.

What was *wrong* with her? Charlotte asked herself angrily. Surely she was long past the age for yearning after the impossible? Surely she had long ago accepted the kind of woman she was? Did she honestly want to be like the Vanessas of this world? Did she honestly want every man she met to assess her only in terms of her sexuality?

Hadn't she decided long, long ago that she was better off the way she was? So why had she experienced that hot flare of resentment when she had watched Oliver smiling at Sophy with a male appreciation she just knew he would never show her?

Damn Oliver Tennant. Until he had arrived to disrupt her life, she had been perfectly happy. She had had a good business, she had been content, and now suddenly both were being threatened.

'What's wrong?' Sheila asked in concern, registering her fierce frown and silence.

'I was just thinking I'd better warn Mrs Higham about Oliver Tennant,' Charlotte lied, her frown deepening as she realised how quickly she had gone from fiercely denying that she would allow Oliver Tennant to put so much as a single foot inside her house, to, not only accepting the fact that he was going to be her lodger, but actually making practical plans for accommodating him.

She chewed bitterly on her already bruised lip, ignoring the pain she was causing herself as she realised how perilously close she had come to actually worrying about the paucity of food in her fridge and cupboards to satisfy the appetite of a large healthy man.

She herself was careful about her diet, although not to the point of obsession. While not a vegetarian, she rarely touched red meat, preferring more easy to digest fish. She still missed the fresh home-grown vegetables she had enjoyed in the days when her father had employed a gardener. Mirthlessly she acknowledged that, if Oliver Tennant's arrival as a competitor affected her business as badly as seemed possible, she could always put her spare time to good use by recultivating the old vegetable garden.

She enjoyed cooking in a modest way, and had even begun to think about trying her hand at breadmaking once her new Aga was installed. Mentally visualising the new kitchen she had planned, she caught herself up with a start, her face suddenly flushing bright pink.

Sheila, who was watching her, and who of course could not see the two dark-haired, blue-eyed children who had materialised so treacherously easily through her imagination, asked anxiously if she was all right.

'Fine,' Charlotte told her briskly, hurriedly escaping from the office before her mind could play any more tricks on her.

On her way over to her solicitor's office to give him the tenancy agreement to look over, she told herself severely that she was losing her grip, and then palliated this harsh denouncement by allowing that the size of her kitchen did lend itself to visions of family rather than single life. She had always loved and wanted children . . . those two could have been any of the children she knew . . . but they hadn't been . . . that dark hair, those blue eyes. She gave a small shudder and closed her mind to any more inadvertent wanderings down such dangerous byways.

Paul's secretary told her that he was free to see her. When she explained the purpose of her call, far from looking surprised as she had expected, he, like Sheila, was full of approval.

How many more people were going to surprise her by telling her how worried they had been at the thought of her living alone? she wondered half an hour later, when Paul had given his approval to the document Oliver had produced.

'I am an adult,' she told him severely as she left. 'I can look after myself, you know.'

'No one's doubting that,' he assured her. 'But these days . . . a woman living alone somewhere so remote. . . Well, it has given me one or two sleepless nights. I've wanted to talk to you about it, but I didn't want to frighten you.'

Frighten her? If only he knew! She was far more frightened by the prospect of having Oliver Tennant living in her home than she was of the remote possibility of someone breaking into it.

She didn't want to risk seeing Oliver Tennant in person again, not until she had managed to have a severe talk with herself about the stupidity of reacting so dangerously to him, and so she sent the signed tenancy agreement round to his office in Sophy's charge and then announced to Sheila that she would be out of the office for the rest of the day, showing prospective clients round some of their properties.

'I'm meeting a couple who are planning to re-
locate here from the north of England. They're retiring and at one time they had family connections
with this area. I think they'll probably go for Cherry
Tree Cottage.'

'Mm. It needs a lot of work doing on it.'

'Yes, but he's taking early retirement and, as I
understand it, isn't in a desperate hurry to move
down here. The house will be close enough to the
village for them. It has a good-sized garden plus a
paddock. Apparently they have grandchildren, who
will be coming to stay, so they'll be able to make
full use of these attic bedrooms.'

'Well, good luck,' Sheila told her.

So far Charlotte had only spoken to the
Markhams over the telephone. When she met them
at the Bull, they proved to be a pleasant couple in
their mid-fifties. Bill Markham had the ruddy skin
of a man used to being outdoors; his wife Anne
seemed a sensible, placid woman, who was plainly
quite happy to go along with her husband's plans
to move them away from their present commuter-
belt home to a more rural area.

They had done their homework on the area well,
Charlotte discovered, as they set off in her Volvo
to view the first property. They were the type of
client she most enjoyed dealing with—discerning,
without being obsessed with finding a property
which matched some impossible dream. She was
not surprised when, at the end of the day, Bill
Markham asked her if they could contact her in the
morning with a view to revisiting three of the five
properties they had seen.

As she had expected, both he and his wife had been drawn to Cherry Tree Cottage, which was a good-sized family house on the outskirts of a sleepy village. It had a wonderful garden, which was now rather neglected, its present owner being an old lady in her early eighties who was selling the house to go and live with her younger sister. It did have certain disadvantages—the roof was thatched, it had no mains drainage, and there was no central heating—but the price was a fair one, and Bill and Anne Markham were young enough to enjoy the challenge of taking on a house which, with some hard work and admittedly some money spent on it, could be made into a very attractive home.

She dropped them outside the Bull, having made arrangements to get in touch with them in the morning. As she started to drive away, she saw Oliver Tennant crossing the car park. She had forgotten for the moment that he too was staying at the pub.

Anxious to get away before he should see her and think that she was deliberately trying to court his attention, she moved the Volvo with less than her usual skill, grating the gears in a way which instantly brought his head up as he focused on her.

Furious with herself, all too conscious of her flushed face, Charlotte wished she had the *savoir-faire* to ignore the fact that he had changed direction and was now walking towards her, and to simply ignore him and drive away.

She couldn't, though. Her father and her school had both been sticklers for good manners and so, gritting her teeth, she stayed where she was until Oliver had reached the car.

As he leaned down towards the open window of the Volvo she caught the clean fresh-air scent of his skin mingled with something else, something alien and male that made her own skin prickle with unexpected heat.

'Thanks for sending the agreement back so quickly,' he said easily. 'I was hoping to have a word with you so that I could make a formal arrangement to move in.'

Her heart was thudding frantically for no reason at all that she could think of, as though it was responding to the unfamiliar dangerous excitement that quickened her pulse.

'You haven't even seen the rooms yet,' Charlotte pointed out, striving to appear cool and business-like. 'They may not be what you're looking for.'

'I'm sure they'll be fine, but, if you're free for half an hour this evening, perhaps I could drive over, see them, and then we can discuss them properly.'

Charlotte looked at him uncertainly. Come round... Why did she feel so overwrought and tense whenever she saw him? She wasn't a teenager any more. He was a physically compelling man, yes, but surely she was well beyond the age of reacting like this to mere physical appeal?

'Is something wrong?' she heard him saying. 'Are you too busy tonight? A date, perhaps?'

Her head shot up, her eyes darkening with anger as she searched his face, wondering if he was de-liberately making fun of her.

He must know, she was sure, that she didn't have
any dates...that there was no man in her life. But
the blue eyes that looked back into hers were free
of any hint of amusement; nor was there anything
in his expression to suggest that he had been making
fun of her.

She was getting too sensitive, she told herself
tiredly. Too self-obsessed. Why should he care one
way or the other about her personal life?

'No...no, this evening will be fine,' she agreed.

His mouth twitched suddenly, the amusement she
had looked for before now lightening the blue eyes.

'I'm flattered that you're looking forward to it
so much,' he told her gravely, but she could hear
the laughter behind the words, and just for a
moment she was tempted to tell him exactly how
she did feel about the prospect of having him as
her lodger, but if she did that good manners would
prompt him to look for accommodation elsewhere
and then Vanessa would crow, believing that she
was the one responsible for his decision.

'Obviously I've got certain reservations,' she told
him as crisply as she could. 'And I'm sure you must
have as well.'

'Are you? Why?'

The question surprised her. She stared at him,
her mouth open, her eyes registering her feelings.

'Well, we don't know one another...and, in view
of the fact that we're business competitors——'

'Ah...you're trying to warn me that you intend
to seduce me and steal all my business secrets, is
that it?'

He was grinning now, a genuine, almost boyish grin that deepened the creases alongside his mouth and sent fans of tiny lines raying out from his eyes, and, looking at him, Charlotte felt that she had never hated anyone more in all her life.

He was laughing at her... making fun of her. A storm of emotion she couldn't control boiled up inside her, and, angrily putting the car in gear, she said fiercely, 'No doubt you think it very funny... the fact that I'm so sexless that it's impossible to imagine me doing any such thing. Well, *I* don't, and if it weren't for the fact that I've already signed that tenancy agreement there'd be no way I'd take you on as a lodger now. You might think it amusing to make fun of people's shortcomings. I don't.'

She was ready to move away, not caring that he was still leaning against the car, when to her shock he reached inside the open window and deftly cut the engine.

While she was still in shock, he said crisply, 'I wasn't making fun of you—far from it—and as for your being sexless...' He was frowning now as he registered her white face and trembling hands.

Charlotte barely heard the sound he made under his breath. Hearing him repeat her own words had devastated her. What had possessed her? Why on earth had she reacted like that... laid herself open to him like that, revealing how much his amusement had hurt her?

She was stunned by her own behaviour. Her deepest private feelings were something she never discussed with anyone, and for her to have voiced them in front of this man who was virtually a stranger...

She felt sick and shaky, disorientated and vaguely light-headed.

'Get out.'

Get out? She focused on the hard-boned male face, absently noting the steely look in the blue eyes. He was angry with her, and no wonder. He didn't want to be burdened with her adolescent emotional soul-baring. What on earth had possessed her? she asked herself again.

'If it weren't for the fact that we're standing in this very public place, I'd be tempted to show you just how wrong you are!'

Charlotte stared at him, unable to believe her ears. He couldn't have meant what she thought he had meant. He wouldn't be implying that he found her desirable.

'I'm going home,' she told him huskily. 'Please move out of the way, so that I can drive.'

'You're not driving anywhere, you little fool. You're in no fit state. Now, are you going to get out of that car under your own steam, or am I going to have to drag you out?'

Something about the way he was looking at her warned that he meant every word he was saying. Shakily, Charlotte released her seatbelt and opened the door. 'I've got to get home,' she protested. Dimly she was aware that she was suffering from some kind of shock, and no wonder after what he had said!

'I'll drive you there.'

'My car——' she protested, but she was already being ushered very firmly across the car park to the parked Jaguar.

'I'll arrange for it to be returned to you.'

'You don't have to do this...' she told him uncertainly, putting her hand to her head. Her head was aching badly. Strange...she hadn't realised she had a headache. Tension-induced, of course. Suddenly, for no reason at all, she felt her eyes start to swim with tears and an awful choking sensation block her throat.

She had stood on her feet for so long, had been independent and self-sufficient for so long that this inner weakness was something she didn't know how to cope with.

Why on earth this particular man should be affecting her like this she had no idea.

'I don't want to go with you,' she told him almost childishly, unaware that she had spoken out loud until he said drily,

'Yes, I know. You don't want anything to do with me, do you, Charlotte? In fact, you don't want anything to do with my sex at all, do you?'

Somehow or other they were both inside his car, and he was fastening her seatbelt while he waited for her answer. She felt shock-waves of sensation burst through her, washing over her body in ever-increasing heat.

'Or is it me personally?' he pressed.

Him personally? For a moment she thought he must have registered her reaction to him, and she gave him a guarded, almost frightened look that made his frown deepen. The shock of what he had said to her was slowly fading, the lump had disappeared from her throat, and when she blinked she discovered that the tears had gone too.

He had caught her off guard, that was all. There had been no real reason for her to get in such a panic . . . to feel so vulnerable.

He was still waiting for a response, and, even though he had now set the car in motion, she knew instinctively that he would continue to press her until he got one.

After the way she had just behaved, she suspected that the last thing he would want to do now was to share her roof, and so there was nothing to be gained from concealing the truth.

'I just don't like being pushed into corners,' she told him restlessly. 'Everyone seems to think I should be pleased to have you lodging with me . . .'

'When in reality it's the last thing you want. Why did you agree, then? Is it just the money?'

She shook her head. 'No,' she admitted. 'It was Vanessa. I didn't want her to think that I was influenced by what she said.'

'Ah, Vanessa. A most unpleasant woman, although I suppose I shouldn't say so.' As though he felt her surprise, he grimaced. 'I feel very sorry for her husband, because, no matter how much he does for her, it will never be enough. I must admit I'm looking forward to moving into my new quarters.'

'To moving in? Oh, but surely——?'

'Surely what I'll do now is the gentlemanly thing and let you off the hook, now that I know you don't want me. I'm afraid not,' he told her calmly.

'I've already wasted far too much time looking for somewhere suitable, and besides, like you, I feel that the kind of comments that Vanessa was making are best refuted by being totally ignored. Which way?' he asked her.

Automatically she told him, and then lapsed into a numb silence as they covered the miles in easy comfort. He was a good driver; the Jaguar was bliss to ride in. It smelled of leather, and the passenger seat seemed to curve itself around her body. Within twenty minutes they were turning into the drive. She saw Oliver frown as he noted the rickety gates and unkempt drive, although all he said when he eventually stopped the car in front of the house was, 'Excellent situation . . . for a family. Do you have much land?'

'An acre of garden and a good-sized paddock,' Charlotte responded automatically.

She never used the front door, keeping it bolted and barred at all times, but now she reflected that perhaps she ought to have new locks put on it so that Oliver could use it. That way she would be decreasing the risks of their paths crossing too frequently. The risks . . . what risks, for heaven's sake?

She saw the way he studied the house as she opened the porch door. When he followed her into the kitchen, she found herself gabbling that she was waiting for the joiner to start work on the new units, and quickly stopped herself. Why on earth was she apologising to him? What did it matter to her what he thought of her home?

But to her surprise he said easily, 'My mother died last year. It was months before I could bring myself to do anything about her house. There's always such a feeling of betrayal and guilt involved in the death of a parent, isn't there? A feeling of reluctance to change anything. I suppose it's all part of the natural healing process. The trouble is that nowadays we're all too geared to the media vision of instant everything to accept that some things take time. Do you miss him?'

'Not really,' Charlotte admitted. 'He wasn't easy to get on with and we weren't really close. I suppose it was guilt that brought me home in the first place, and guilt that kept me here.'

She was surprised to discover how easy it was to admit it to him.

'I'd better show you the rooms,' she said awkwardly, opening the kitchen door and waiting for him to follow her.

In the end she showed him all through the house, and then the garden. He was surprisingly knowledgeable about the latter for a man who lived in London, and when he said quietly, 'Would you mind if I tried my hand at resuscitating your vegetable plot?' Charlotte said the first thing that came into her head.

'But you won't be here long enough. You said six months.'

'Yes, I know. So the garden is out of bounds to me, is it?'

'No...no... Of course not.'

What had she said? She had no intention of sharing her garden with him as well as her home. The trouble with Oliver Tennant was that he never reacted in the way she expected, and so he was constantly catching her off guard. She had no idea why he would want to bother himself with her neglected vegetable garden, but now it seemed she had given him permission to do so, just as she had tacitly agreed to accept him as her lodger.

There were still various minor details to sort out. It was almost eight o'clock before he finally got up to leave.

Charlotte walked out with him to his car. As he opened the door he turned round. Instinctively she stepped back from him.

'By the way,' he said calmly, 'there's just one more thing.'

Charlotte waited patiently, and was stunned when his head descended towards her own and he said quietly in her ear, 'Look at me, Charlotte. I don't think you're sexless, far from it. Shall I prove it to you?'

The shock of his words immobilised her for just long enough for his hand to settle firmly against her jaw and gently turn her face towards his own, so that his mouth could feather slowly against her skin until it came to rest against hers.

A shudder of shock racked her as her senses registered the moist warmth of his lips and their gentle persuasive movement against her own. Her eyes, wide open and dazed, stared into his. She couldn't believe this was happening, but it was. His free hand was resting on her waist, propelling her forward to close the gap between their bodies. She could feel the heat coming off his skin—or was it her own flesh that was giving off that warmth? The hand on her jaw stroked her throat and then her nape, the long fingers burrowing under her hair, while her pulse jerked frantically and her heart pounded in her chest. And all the time his mouth was moving on hers, slowly, subtly, seductively, so that her insides were turning fluid and molten and she was automatically obeying the silent command of his mouth and responding to the growing pressure of his kiss.

His kiss...he was kissing her! Frantically Charlotte pushed him away, standing back from him as he released her immediately. A hundred questions clamoured on her lips, but she couldn't voice any of them, couldn't ask why he had done such an extraordinary thing. She already knew, of course. He felt sorry for her. Well, she didn't want his pity, nor his kisses. Nausea turned her stomach to ice. Had it really come to that...that a man kissed her out of pity?

'Charlotte——'

'Please don't ever do that again,' she told him fiercely. 'I don't need your...your kisses, and I don't want them.'

Before he could say anything she turned on her heel and almost ran back into the house. When she reached the kitchen she was shaking. What an appalling thing to have happened.

And why had it happened? It had happened because she had behaved stupidly.

She shuddered now, remembering that moment in the car park when she had blurted out those fateful words. A small groan broke the silence of her kitchen. How could she have behaved like that ... spoken like that? It had been tantamount to asking him to deny her words.

Was that *why* she had said them? Because a part of her had known that out of compassion he must reject them?

She winced at the thought, filled with a humiliating awareness of what Oliver Tennant must be thinking about her. What she could not understand was why, after what she had said, he had not changed his mind about lodging with her.

Telling herself it was pointless to go over and over the whole thing endlessly looking for explanations and reasons, she acknowledged that the only way she was going to be able to live with her folly was to behave as though it had never happened—and that included behaving as though that kiss had never happened as well. And yet almost she was unable to resist the impulse to touch her fingers to her mouth, as though in doing so there was some way she could recapture the sensation of his moving against it.

Angry with herself, she snatched her hand away. She had far more important things to do than to stand here agonising over a kiss given in pity. Far, far more.

CHAPTER SIX

'GOOD, so you are in after all. I've been knocking on this door for ages!' Vanessa exclaimed in an aggrieved voice as Charlotte drew back the final bolt on the front door and opened it.

Once she realised who was standing outside, Charlotte wished she had left the door closed. 'I don't use the front door much,' she told her unwanted visitor, adding coolly, 'Is Adam with you?'

'No, I thought it best that we have our little chat alone.'

A tingle of apprehension ran down Charlotte's spine. It was most unusual for Vanessa to come round to see her, and she suspected she knew what, or rather who had brought her.

Closing the door and heading for the kitchen, Charlotte was conscious of Vanessa's deprecating study of the house.

'I can't understand why you simply don't just sell this place,' she sniffed as they walked into the kitchen and sat down. 'It's far too large for one person, and it needs a fortune spending on it to bring it up to scratch. You'd be better off with a small purpose-built flat. After all, it's not as though you're ever likely to marry, is it?'

The words, which only echoed her own private thoughts—thoughts which until recently she had found quite acceptable—now jarred, conjuring up an unwanted memory of those two dark-haired, blue-eyed imaginary children.

'Whether or not I marry has no bearing on where I choose to make my home,' she told Vanessa lightly, trying not to allow the other woman to get under her skin. 'This house has been my home for all of my life. I may sell it, I may not. I haven't made up my mind as yet.'

'Oh, come on, Charlotte. There's no need to pretend with me. There's only one reason you're hanging on to it and we both know what that is,' Vanessa accused nastily. 'The moment you heard that Oliver was looking for accommodation you made up your mind, didn't you? I suppose I shouldn't blame you. After all, how often does a woman in your position—single, plain, over twenty-five—get the opportunity to insinuate herself so closely into the life of an eligible, handsome man? As I said, I can understand perfectly well why you approached Oliver with this ludicrous idea of yours that he move in here with you, but, as one of your oldest friends, I felt that I must warn you. Even Adam agreed with me that in the circumstances——'

'Adam? You've discussed this with Adam?'

Immediately she saw the triumph in Vanessa's eyes, Charlotte regretted her sharp words.

'Well, he *is* my husband, and I thought as a man he would be able to give me a man's view of things. I must say it was no different really from mine. Of course, he put it rather more . . . well, bluntly than I would have done. ''You know what people will say when they find out he's living there, don't you?'' he said to me. ''They're bound to think that there's something going on. And of course they're bound to feel sorry for Charlie. And I suppose you can't blame her...he's an attractive man.''' Vanessa lifted her eyebrows. 'Attractive—I ask you! Men can be so blind, can't they? But then Adam, poor dear, would be the last person to recognise Oliver's very male appeal——'

Growing steadily angrier as she listened to Vanessa, Charlotte cut through her monologue to demand curtly, 'Just why have you come here, Vanessa?'

'Why? Well, to warn you of course, darling. Look, I know how you must feel, how tempted you must be to ignore the facts and allow yourself to imagine... Well, you wouldn't be human, would you, if you hadn't imagined just what Oliver would be like in bed? But as your friend... Well, think about it, darling,' she purred, ignoring the grim silence emanating from her 'friend'. 'What on earth could a man like Oliver really see in a woman like you? I mean, let's be realistic...how many men have there been in your life since your engagement was broken?' She paused delicately, like a cat toying with an injured mouse, Charlotte reflected tiredly.

All at once she had had more than enough.

'Vanessa, I'm not sure what you're trying to imply, but I should tell you now that Oliver Tennant is moving in here as a temporary lodger and nothing more. He means nothing to me other than a source of some additional income to help with the running expenses of this house while I decide what to do with it. If people choose to think differently, well, there is very little I can do about it. However, I am sure that those people who know me as well as you do will realise as you have done the implausibility of there being any relationship between us which is not strictly business.'

'Ah, yes, that's another thing I felt I ought to warn you about,' Vanessa pounced. 'My dear, have you thought why Oliver has chosen to come and live here with you? Why, you heard me offering him our guest room rent-free. Think about it, my dear. What possible advantage could there be to his staying here? In the business sense, of course.'

'What is it you're trying to say, Vanessa?' Charlotte demanded frigidly.

Vanessa pouted.

'Surely you can guess? Oliver is your business rival—what better way for him to completely undermine your business than by moving in here with you and, well . . . pretending that he is attracted to you? I just thought I ought to warn you,' she added virtuously. 'And so did Adam. I mean, I suppose in time you'd have realised the truth for yourself, but of course by then it might be far too late. We women can be such fools where our hearts are concerned, can't we?'

If she didn't get rid of Vanessa soon she was either going to scream or be sick, Charlotte recognised. She had never been so angry in her life. How dared Vanessa walk in and suggest . . .? Did she really think she was so stupid, so desperate, that she would allow herself to be deceived in the way Vanessa was suggesting? She had far too much sense.

Or had she? That kiss this evening—a gesture of pity, of compassion, from a man who had unexpectedly shown her that he had awareness of the feelings of others, that had broken down the barriers she had put up against his sex. Or had it had an ulterior, far less altruistic motive?

Could she have been mistaken about his motives? Surely not? That unguarded comment of hers about her lack of sexual appeal hadn't been something he could have known she was going to say. Even so, an extra burden of anxiety had been added to the ones she already carried.

She had no illusions about Oliver's determination to establish his agency here. He had claimed that there was room for both of them, and so there was, but she had suspected all along that a man with his drive would never be satisfied with merely a share of the market. Hitherto, though, she had assumed that the competition between them would be conducted on a strictly business footing.

Now Vanessa had succeeded in sowing fresh doubts in her mind. Was his decision to come and live here all part of a carefully planned campaign? Had he, on hearing that she was looking for a lodger, deliberately decided to turn that fact to his own use?

Did he intend to deceive her into believing that something more than a business relationship could be established between them? Did he intend, once having won her confidence, to use her vulnerability to him to destroy her completely?

Charlotte shivered a little and Vanessa's sharp eyes noticed the betraying gesture. She smiled to herself and stood up. 'Naturally, as your friend, I had to warn you. I mean, people aren't stupid, are they? Everyone will soon start putting two and two together—especially the men.' She rolled her eyes. 'You know what they can be like. Before you know where you are, they'll be sniggering about you behind your back, making crude jokes. If I were you I shouldn't waste a moment in telling Oliver that you've changed your mind,' she added carefully. 'After all, he'll soon find somewhere else to live.'

Immediately Charlotte realised the real purpose of Vanessa's visit. Smiling evenly, she said sweetly, 'You never give up, do you, Vanessa? But I'm afraid it's too late. You see, Oliver and I have already signed a tenancy agreement. I can't change my mind. However, I do appreciate your concern. Not that it was necessary,' she added carelessly. 'I'm not as gullible as you seem to think.'

She was still seething with bitterness and resentment long after she had got rid of Vanessa. Her poisoned words had done their work well, dripping venom into Charlotte's thoughts, making her question just what had motivated Oliver to be so nice to her... to kiss her.

If only Vanessa had known how Charlotte really felt about accepting Oliver as her lodger, and that it was her interference and advice that had made it impossible for Charlotte to draw back from the agreement with him!

That knowledge brought Charlotte a small measure of comfort as she reflected grimly on the less pleasant aspects of Vanessa's visit. Even knowing that Vanessa had deliberately been trying to wound her didn't lessen her own feeling of inner disquiet.

She was already far too vulnerable to Oliver, far too aware of him. That kiss... But no, she had told herself she wasn't going to think about it, to dwell on it...that she was sensibly going to put it out of her mind and forget about it completely.

However, that was easier said than done. In the morning she was still brooding over Vanessa's nastiness, and Sheila, watching her frown, asked her quietly, 'Is something wrong?'

'No,' Charlotte lied automatically, and then admitted, 'Yes...there is. Vanessa called round yesterday and had another go at trying to persuade me not to take on Oliver as a lodger.' She pulled a face. 'Oh, she pretended it was concern for me that prompted her visit. She was full of "Adam says" and "Adam agrees with me". She went on and on about the danger of people gossiping. You can imagine the sort of thing.'

'Yes, I can,' Sheila agreed, and then said disparagingly, 'That woman is such a bitch. She's jealous of you, of course.'

Charlotte stared at her. 'Vanessa, jealous of me? Oh, come on. She despises me. And, let's be honest, what do I have that she could possibly envy? Her own sex may realise what she's really like, but men are always taken in by that sugary appearance.' Charlotte made another face. 'She's attractive, she's got a wonderful husband, two healthy children, a lovely home.'

'Yes, and we all know which of those is the most important to her,' Sheila said shrewdly. 'Vanessa is an avaricious woman. Wealth, social position, possessions—those are what matter to her. Those and having her vanity constantly stroked by some admiring male. But she's not getting any younger, and women like her have only one asset to use as a trade-off for what they want from life. I dare say Adam is devoted to her, but without him she'd have nothing. She's like a bloodsucker sinking her claws into a man stupid enough to love her and wealthy enough to provide her with all the things she wants, but if she ever loses that man... That's why she envies you, Charlotte—because you're not vulnerable the way she is. You're independent, you have your own career, your own home.'

'But I'm alone,' Charlotte said fiercely, not realising what she was giving away. 'Vanessa has a husband...children.'

'Whom she'd dump in a second if a wealthier man than Adam ever came along and offered her marriage and access to his bank account. She resents you and tries to put you down because inwardly she knows you're worth ten of her. And as for people gossiping about you and Oliver—that's a ludicrous suggestion.'

'Yes, I know,' Charlotte agreed a little hollowly. 'I don't know why I let her get to me really.'

The phone rang and Sheila picked it up.

While she was speaking, Charlotte busied herself with her own work. Once she had replaced the receiver, Sheila came over to her desk and announced, 'That was old Mrs Birtles. You know—she owns Hadley Court.'

'Yes, of course. It's a beautiful place.'

'Mmm. Well, it seems she's thinking of putting it up for sale. She wondered if you'd care to go round and see her. Oh, and by the way, she said to tell you that she'd approached Mr Tennant as well, and that in fairness to both of you she thought she ought to see you both at the same time. This afternoon at two o'clock, to be precise. Perhaps she'll invite you to challenge one another to a duel,' Sheila suggested, grinning at Charlotte's expression. 'She is supposed to be rather eccentric.'

'Thanks very much. Did she give you directions? I've a vague idea where it is.'

'She did and here they are,' Sheila told her, giving her a piece of paper.

'Mm. Should be easy enough to find,' Charlotte agreed, reading through them. 'Two o'clock. Let's just hope the Volvo doesn't let me down again.'

'Have you made any decision on a new car yet?' Sheila asked her.

'Mm, I think so—only it isn't one car, it's two. I've decided that there's no point in being unduly pessimistic about the effect Oliver Tennant is going to have on our business, and so as well as buying a new car for myself I've bought one for the office as well. You and Sophy will be able to use it.'

She laughed when she saw Sheila's face and added warningly, 'You'll have to come to some arrangement between you about who has the use of it out of business hours.' She rummaged in her open briefcase and extracted some papers. 'Here are the colour charts. I'm opting for the dark grey.'

'Oh, look at that red!' Sheila enthused, avidly studying the brochures Charlotte had given her until the telephone rang again.

When she replaced the receiver she was frowning. 'That was Dan Pearce from Rush Farm. He wanted to know if anyone has shown any interest in those semis yet.'

Charlotte frowned too. 'He told me he was going to instruct Oliver—perhaps he's changed his mind.'

'Or perhaps Oliver told him the same thing you did—that he'd never get the kind of money he's looking for unless he applies for planning consent and sells them both together. He sounded very surly.'

'He is very surly. He hasn't lived here long himself, has he? He inherited that farm, didn't he?'

'Yes, he lives there on his own. His wife left him shortly after they moved in. There was a bit of a scandal about it at the time. Some suggestion that he had been violent with her.' Sheila was looking concerned. 'Look, do you think you ought to see him on your own?'

'Oh, Sheila, for heaven's sake!' Charlotte said impatiently. 'I admit that the man isn't very pleasant but, really, you're letting your imagination run away with you. Have you got his number? I'll give him a ring and arrange to go out there and see him again. After all,' she added grimly, 'we can't afford to turn our backs on potential business, can we?'

Charlotte had a busy morning. Bill and Anne Markham, after going round three of the previous day's properties a second time, announced, as she had hoped they would, that they wanted to make an offer for Cherry Tree Cottage.

Having assured them that she would put their offer to the owner and get back to them as quickly as she could, Charlotte ate a quick sandwich lunch in her car, washed down by a cup of coffee from her thermos, before checking that her hair was neat, and reapplying her lipstick before heading for her two o'clock appointment at Hadley Court.

She was less than half a mile away from the house, and nicely on time, when disaster struck. There was a short queue of traffic on the minor road, waiting to pull out at a junction. She was stuck behind four other cars, and, while she sat waiting for her turn to filter into the mainstream of traffic, the Volvo's engine suddenly died on her.

No amount of frantic turning of the ignition key would restart the motor, and finally, flustered and bad-tempered, she climbed out of the car and, with the help of a fellow motorist, pushed the Volvo safely to the side of the road.

It was now ten past two. Damn! Damn! she swore furiously. She just could not afford to lose the kind of business Hadley Court represented. Looking down grimly at her almost new court shoes, she acknowledged there was only one thing for it.

It was a pleasant spring afternoon, but she was in no mood to appreciate the warmth of the sunshine or the beauty of her surroundings when she finally reached the gates to Hadley Court.

Ahead of her, parked on the gravel forecourt, was Oliver's Jaguar, and gritting her teeth, she set off to walk down the drive, wincing as her shoes continually filled with the small chippings and had to be emptied.

When she finally reached the imposing front door it was half-past two. A light breeze had tousled her hair, and whipped colour into her cheeks, she felt untidy and hot, and not at all in the right frame of mind to present the kind of professional appearance she wanted to present.

The door opened even before she reached for the knocker.

'I'm sorry I'm late,' she apologised to the woman who opened it. 'I have an appointment with Mrs Birtles. Charlotte——'

'Yes, yes . . . please come in. We saw you walking down the drive and Mr Tennant told me who you were. I'd no idea you intended to walk,' she added vaguely. 'I'm May Birtles, by the way,' she added, leaving Charlotte to follow her across the stone-flagged dimly lit hall.

Instinctively, Charlotte cast a professional glance over her surroundings. The house had a Queen Anne façade, but here in the panelling adorning the walls, and the stone-flagged floor, was evidence of an older building.

An intricately carved staircase led up to the upper storeys of the house, and, although Charlotte would have loved to have stopped and studied it in more detail, she followed Mrs Birtles, who opened a pair of beautiful panelled double doors into another room.

At first the sunshine streaming in through the windows blinded Charlotte to her surroundings. She had a confused impression of rich brocades in soft faded colours, of a highly polished marquetry floor covered with delicate silky rugs, of immense gilt-framed portraits of sober-clothed individuals, of a scent of some kind of sharp, fresh pot-pourri, and huge bowls of freshly cut flowers, and last of all of Oliver Tennant, standing in front of one of the windows.

He was frowning, Charlotte recognised, when her eyes had become accustomed to the brilliance of the sunshine.

Initially his terse, 'Are you all right?' confused her a little until Mrs Birtles explained.

'Mr Tennant was concerned about you. He told me that something must have happened to you to make you late for our appointment. I did offer to take him round the house without waiting for you, but he insisted on waiting.'

While Charlotte absorbed this, she was staring at Oliver, unable to comprehend that the grim look of concern tightening his mouth was actually on her account. 'My car broke down,' she told them both. 'Luckily I was only half a mile or so away, so, after someone helped me to push it out of the way, I walked here.'

She heard the sound Oliver made under his breath. 'You could have asked me for a lift,' he told her sharply.

Charlotte stared at him. Ask *him* for a lift...?

She could tell from the way Mrs Birtles was smiling so approvingly at him that the older woman was completely bowled over by him. No prizes for guessing whom she would appoint as her agent, Charlotte reflected sourly, refusing to allow the warmth which had developed inside her when she had recognised his concern to grow.

'Well, now that you are both here,' Mrs Birtles was saying placidly, apparently unaware of Charlotte's antipathy towards her fellow agent, 'shall we make a start?'

The house was large and rambling and, in addition to selling it with the several acres of land that went with it, Mrs Birtles also wanted to dispose of a large number of pieces of antique furniture.

'I'm going to live abroad,' she told them both. 'I have no one to leave the house to. It's a family home really. My husband inherited it from a distant cousin and we lived here for almost twenty years. When he died...well, I have a sister living in Florida who's invited me to join her.'

Oliver, who had been inspecting a piece of furniture, turned round and asked her, 'Is the house listed?'

Mrs Birtles frowned. 'No...no, it isn't. Why do you ask?'

Charlotte thought she knew. A listed building was protected and could not be altered in any way without proper consent. A listing protected a property, but sometimes put off prospective purchasers, especially of a house this size. A developer who might be interested in purchasing the house for the value of its land, with the intention of destroying the house and using the land to build a new estate, wouldn't be interested if he knew the house was protected by a listing.

Charlotte had stopped listening to Mrs Birtles and Oliver; heaven alone knew why Mrs Birtles had asked her here. It was painfully obvious that she was going to commission Oliver. Fair-mindedly, Charlotte acknowledged to herself that Oliver with his contacts in London would probably be able to effect a sale much more easily than she would herself. This property was way outside the normal type of house she dealt with. It would need special-ised handling, ads in such publications as *Country Life*, special brochures. It should perhaps be sold by auction—certainly an auction of the furniture Mrs Birtles wanted to dispose of would bring in more money than private sales.

She heard Mrs Birtles saying something about terms, and switched her attention back to their conversation.

'I think you'll find that both Miss Spencer and I operate a similar scale of charges.'

Charlotte stared at him. This wasn't what she had expected. She had been waiting for Oliver to go all out to sell *himself* and *his* services to Mrs Birtles. Instead he was saying something about Charlotte's having the advantage over him in local knowledge, and then he paused, as though giving her the opportunity to take advantage of her cue.

No, this wasn't what she had expected at all. Where was the hard-driving, ambitious, un-scrupulous sales technique she had expected? Where was the sharp cutting edge of the London-trained businessman?

Honesty had always been one of Charlotte's strongest virtues. It niggled at her now, forcing her to confess to Mrs Birtles, 'Lovely though your home is, I've got to admit I've never handled this kind of sale before.' She looked instinctively towards Oliver as though seeking his support. 'Mr Tennant is probably far better placed to advise you on the best way of achieving a sale.'

She saw a faint hint of respect tinging Oliver's eyes. Had he really expected her to behave less professionally and honestly than he had himself? Now he spoke again.

'To be honest with you, Mrs Birtles, this is a prestigious property, and would be best handled in conjunction with one of the agents who specialise in handling such properties on a countrywide basis.

'As it happens, I know one of the partners in one of these agencies, and I'd be delighted to arrange for him to come down here and see you.'

'No,' Mrs Birtles told him firmly. 'My husband always believed in giving his business to local people and I have carried on that tradition.'

'Well, then, in that case,' Oliver said with a smile, 'perhaps I could suggest that you appoint both Miss Spencer and myself as joint agents. That way you could have the benefit of our joint expertise.'

'Joint agents...that's a marvellous idea,' Mrs Birtles enthused, while Oliver looked across at Charlotte, one eyebrow lifted as he awaited her comments.

Joint agents... That was the last thing she had expected him to suggest. There was a hard lump of emotion in her throat. Honesty compelled her to admit that he had probably far more experience in this field than she did herself, and he must know that, and yet he had still suggested a joint agency.

She swallowed and said huskily, 'We'll both do our best to obtain a good sale for you, Mrs Birtles.'

There were various arrangements to be made. The items to be sold would have to be catalogued. Charlotte had had experience of this while working for an auction house during her university holidays, and offered to take over this chore.

'It will give me an opportunity to teach Sophy how to prepare a catalogue,' she explained, when Oliver said quietly to her,

'Cataloguing is a bit of a chore—are you sure?'

'Sophy is working for *you*?' He frowned.

'Just on a part-time basis at the moment,' Charlotte told him. 'To fit in with the twins.' Pride forbade her to add that Sophy's job would be more temporary than she had planned if he succeeded in taking the major part of her business.

He was still frowning. 'I shouldn't have thought your business merited taking on extra staff at the moment.'

Mrs Birtles had left the room to instruct her housekeeper to bring them all some coffee, and so there was no one to overhear them as Charlotte forgot how grateful she had been to him not five minutes before and hissed bitterly, 'What do you know about my business? For your information, until you decided to open up in this area——' She bit her lip, suddenly aware of what she was giving away, but it was too late.

Oliver was saying softly, 'You took Sophy on because you knew, if she didn't have a job, she'd lose her home.'

'Don't be ridiculous,' Charlotte denied. 'I'm a businesswoman, not a charitable organisation.'

There was no opportunity for them to say any more because Mrs Birtles had returned.

After they had finished their coffee, Charlotte offered to drive over the following week to take the necessary measurements on a day when Mrs Birtles had informed her that the house would be empty.

When Oliver shook his head, Charlotte stared at him. Didn't he trust her to do the job properly?

'I don't think it's a good idea for you to come to an empty house, especially one that's so remote,' he told her calmly. When she started to object, he said quietly, 'Yes, perhaps I am over-reacting a little, but you forget, I'm from London. Few agents there can forget that Suzy Lamplugh disappeared after ostensibly showing a prospective client around an empty property.'

Charlotte stared at him, confused by the conflicting emotions she was experiencing. He was so compassionate, so caring, and she was so unused to this kind of protective concern from anyone, least of all from a man.

'But I shan't *be* showing anyone around,' she told him when she had got herself under control and subdued the sudden rush of helpless pleasure his concern brought.

'No, but you will be here alone. I'm glad you've taken Sophy on. Not just for her sake, but with two of you working together it should be much safer for you both.'

Charlotte opened her mouth to correct his misapprehension that she took Sophy with her when showing prospective customers around properties, and then closed it again.

Half an hour later, when they had completed a tour of the gardens, and Oliver offered to drive her back to town, Charlotte found herself agreeing easily and with a sudden sharp, exhilarating rush of pleasure.

She *wanted* to be with him, she recognised as he opened the car door for her. She wanted to be with him; she wanted to have him looking at her the way he was doing right now, smiling into her eyes and making her feel as though she were something fragile and precious, as though...

Stop it, she warned herself. Just because he's being friendly, it doesn't mean that... That what? That he found her attractive... desirable... What on earth was she thinking? Of course he didn't.

He had kissed her, had held her. But he was a Londoner, a city dweller, sophisticated and worldly—kisses were common currency in his world and meant nothing.

Nothing at all.

CHAPTER SEVEN

'IT WAS generous of you to suggest to Mrs Birtles that she appoint us as joint agents,' Charlotte said hesitantly.

She had been conscious of the occasional glances Oliver gave her as he drove, and her own conscience prodded her now into thanking him for what he had done.

'Not generous at all,' he replied promptly. 'Just good business practice.' As though he had felt her stiffen and withdraw from him, he added easily, 'You've got entirely the wrong idea about me, Charlotte. I have no intention of trying to usurp your place in the business community, but this area is growing fast, and I honestly believe there is room for both of us——'

'You aren't planning to stay here,' Charlotte broke in. 'You just want to drain the area dry while there's a boom on, and then you'll move out.'

'No.' His response was sharp and decisive. 'It's true that originally when my partner and I decided to go our separate ways I wasn't sure if I could afford the luxury of a country office as well as one in London, but I like it here. I've decided to sell out my share of the London office. I know someone who's keen to buy me out—for a very generous sum. In fact, that's one of the reasons I wanted——' He broke off to overtake a man on a bike, and Charlotte wondered what he had been about to say.

'I'm tired of London life,' he told her when he had successfully passed the wobbling bike. 'I've reached a stage in my life when I want to put down roots, establish a firm base.'

Marry and have children, Charlotte wondered as her heart suddenly thumped frantically. But of course those were questions she could not ask. Instead she returned to a subject which was still plaguing her a little.

'I'm not sure I've got the expertise to deal with a property like Mrs Birtles'.'

'Don't you want to do it?' Oliver asked her.

Charlotte stared at him and then said firmly, 'Of course I do, but I felt I ought to be honest with you ... I don't think it will be easy to sell. Even with the influx of London buyers. Had you thought of any kind of valuation?'

'Yes,' he told her, and named a sum that made her gasp a little.

'As much as that?'

'More,' he told her crisply, 'if it was sold to a group enterprise.'

'A group enterprise?' Charlotte faltered.

'Mm. You know, one of these conglomerates that specialise in turning large old properties into desirable smaller units. The fact that it isn't listed would make the necessary planning permission easier to acquire, of course.'

'You mean destroy the house and build an estate,' Charlotte fired up immediately. Suddenly all her pleasure in his company, in his treatment of her as an equal in matters of business, had turned to ashes in her mouth. She had thought that, like her, he had felt a genuine desire to find exactly the right buyer for the house—someone who would love and cherish it as it deserved to be loved and cherished—and now here he was casually talking about its destruction.

How wrong she had been. She could have sworn as she watched him gently smoothing his palm against the polished wood of the carved banister that he had felt the same way about the house as she had done, but it had all been just an act.

'That's sacrilege,' she told him bitterly, and then added, 'That was why you asked Mrs Birtles if it was listed, wasn't it? Oh, God! Stop the car!' she demanded furiously.

'What?'

'I want to get out—out of your car, and out of any joint selling agreement. I thought you felt as I do, that you wanted to find the right purchaser for the house, when instead——'

'I do,' he interrupted her ruthlessly, 'but you seemed to be forgetting that our first responsibility isn't to the house but to Mrs Birtles. It's obvious that she is having difficulty maintaining the house now that her husband is dead. It's her sole investment.'

Charlotte blinked at him, suddenly and shamingly aware of how much she had missed. She had seen the house and fallen in love with it, but now he made her remember the small touches of shabbiness she had seen but not really registered.

'I suppose you're saying that it will be much easier to find a conglomerate buyer than a private one.'

'Yes,' he agreed emotionlessly. 'But that doesn't mean that a private buyer isn't possible. You know, you'd find life much less fraught if you learned to trust people a little, Charlotte. You're always so ready to believe the worst of others.'

A dark flush stained her skin. His accusation was justified, but that didn't make hearing it any easier.

'I'm sorry if I misjudge you,' she said stiffly.

'Are you?' The look he gave her made her feel uncomfortable, guilty in some way. 'I've got to go up to London for a couple of days, to finalise things with the buyer of my agency there. While I'm there I'll have a word with a couple of people I know— see if they know of anyone who might be interested in the house, strictly off the record.'

'I suppose the best thing will be to auction it,' Charlotte suggested tiredly.

Oliver had ripped the veils of naïveté from her eyes. Every word he had said to her had been true. They did owe it to their client to get the best possible price for her, but she could not bear to think of the house being destroyed.

'Possibly,' Oliver agreed, and then changed the subject, saying, 'I was wondering if it would be convenient for me to move my things into your place tonight, then I could get an early start for London in the morning.'

There was no real reason for her to object. It was crazy to feel suddenly as though the ground was falling away under her feet, as though she wanted to protest that things were happening far too fast for her, that she needed more time...

'The men started work on the kitchen today,' she warned him. 'Everywhere will be in a bit of a mess.'

'I only want somewhere to sleep tonight. And I'll be gone early in the morning.'

They were approaching the town now, and after she had said quietly, 'Very well, then, if you're sure you still want to go ahead,' he gave her a sharp look, but said nothing for a few seconds as he negotiated the traffic.

'What will you do about your car?' he asked her as he swung into the empty town square. There was no market today, and plenty of car parking spaces.

'I'll ring the garage and see if they can keep it going for me until the new one is delivered,' she told him wryly.

'Mmm. Well, you're perfectly welcome to use this while I'm in London, if you'd care to. My insurance does cover other drivers.'

Use this? Charlotte stared at him, unable to believe her ears, and then said shakily, 'Good heavens, I couldn't possibly. What if anything should happen to it?' She looked in awe at the immaculate upholstery and gleaming bodywork.

Perhaps he had heard the note of regret in her voice because, instead of accepting her refusal, he said easily, 'It's only a car, you know—and besides, I've every confidence in your driving.'

Charlotte looked at him. Was this all a part of the softening-up process Vanessa had mentioned, the deliberate and ruthless clinical sabotage of her defences?

This afternoon she had been stunned by his generosity, by his business ethics, so very, very different from what she had imagined. He had seemed so honest, so direct, so completely without any ulterior motive... Was she being too gullible, too trusting?

'Look, I'll leave you the keys and then it's up to you,' she heard him saying.

She protested uncertainly, 'But won't you need it...to get to the station?'

'I'll use a taxi. Much safer than leaving it in some station car park all day.'

He had stopped now. All she had to do was to get out, thank him for the lift and arrange for him to move in his things, and yet as she opened the car door she felt a sharp reluctance to leave.

Firmly quelling it, she got out. This was ridiculous. Any more of this foolishness and she'd be in danger of falling in love with the man.

Falling in love... She froze as the shock of it iced through her. Falling in love with a man like Oliver Tennant. She couldn't be so foolish, could she? Could she...?

Could she?

Unaware of the way Oliver was frowning after her, she got shakily to her feet and headed for her office.

'Well, come on. How did it go?' Sheila asked her excitedly.

Almost absently Charlotte explained how they had been appointed joint agents.

'Well, I must say that was very generous of Oliver Tennant,' Sheila approved.

'Yes,' Charlotte agreed vaguely, unaware of the look of concern that crossed the older woman's face at her lack of enthusiasm. Her insides felt like jelly. She badly wanted to crawl away somewhere where she could be alone to sit and think. In love with Oliver Tennant... It was ridiculous. It couldn't be possible. She had only seen him on half a dozen or so occasions. And there had never once been anything in his manner towards her to encourage such crazy emotions.

She tried to remember if she had felt like this when she had first met Gordon. But that had been different. Their relationship had grown slowly. Their decision to get engaged had been made after a good deal of mutual consideration of their aims in life, and then, when she had told Gordon that she intended to give up her London career to return home, the ending of their engagement had come after equally mature discussions.

Never at any time had Gordon made her feel the way she felt when she was with Oliver.

Without knowing she had done so, she had linked her fingers together, gripping them tightly as she tried to fight off the immensity of her despair. If only she had realised what was happening to her before she had agreed to take him as a lodger. How on earth was she going to endure living so intimately with him?

She would just *have* to endure it, she told herself firmly. After all, it would not be for long. Six months. *Six months*... It had taken her far less

than six *weeks* to fall in love with him. She could
only pray that her love was of the virulent and short-
lived type that would quickly burn itself out like a
tropical fever. It was so out of character for her to
feel like this ... so ... so unsuitable and indignified.
She was a businesswoman who had long ago recognised in her lack of sexual appeal the enormity
of the barrier between her and the things she had
once wanted from life: a husband, children, the
kind of family life she herself had craved as a child
and never had.

Equally she had recognised the danger of
allowing herself to believe that her idealised daydreams of that kind of family life were anything
other than exactly that; relationships, marriage,
children—all required a one-hundred-and-fifty-per-
cent input from all parties concerned, and even then
they so often failed.

How long ago was it now since she had first consoled herself with the knowledge that she was
probably better off on her own, that she had a good
life, good friends ... that she had the enjoyment of
her friends' children without the heartaches ...
that, with her own lack of a strong physical response to those men who did ask her out, it was
probably just as well that the romantic, idealistic
side of her nature made it impossible for her to
settle for a relationship which could not match up
to her ideals?

Now, when she had long ago accepted that the
kind of man she had once dreamed of did not exist,
she had met him ... or was she simply allowing
herself to be blinded to reality? Was Oliver Tennant

the compassionate, caring man he seemed, or was Vanessa right? Was he simply going to use her for his own ends?

'Did you have a word with Oliver about Dan Pearce, to see if he had appointed him?' Sheila asked her, breaking into her thoughts.

Charlotte had forgotten all about the farmer. She frowned and said crisply, 'No, I didn't.'

Seeing her friend's expression, she added firmly, 'Look, *I* might not like the man, Sheila, but that doesn't mean I can afford to turn away his business. If he chose to come back to us, well, then that's our good fortune. I'd better give him a ring and arrange to go out and see him again.'

It was half an hour before she got through to the farmer. He was just as truculent with her on this occasion as he had been the last time she saw him, but eventually Charlotte managed to make arrangements to go out and see him.

'He must have changed his mind and realised that the only way he'll get a good price is by selling the semis together. Oh, and while I remember, I've promised to do an inventory for a catalogue for auctioning some of Mrs Birtles' furniture. I'm going to take Sophy with me...give her an idea of how to do an inventory.'

'Was the house lovely?' Sheila asked wistfully.

'Beautiful,' Charlotte told her. 'The kind of place everyone dreams of owning. I only hope we can find a buyer for it who will appreciate it.'

A frown furrowed her forehead. Oliver had been right when he'd said their first duty was to their client. Perhaps it was idealistic of her to hope that they could find a sole buyer for the house able to meet its price . . . someone who wanted to live in the house and not destroy or develop it.

'Something wrong?' Sheila asked sympathetically.

Charlotte shook her head. She knew that, had her father been alive, he would have agreed with every word Oliver had said. Her father had often accused her of being too sentimental.

'No, not really. I was just wondering if I ought to leave a bit early. Oliver is moving in tonight, and the kitchen people started today.'

Sheila laughed. 'Yes, I think you should. What about your car, though?'

'I've rung the garage to order the two new ones, and they've promised me a loan car until they can provide them. I'm still not sure about that bright red,' she teased Sheila. 'Isn't that supposed to be a dangerous colour?'

'So what?' Sheila retaliated. 'At my age, I think I'm entitled to live a little dangerously.'

Was that what was happening to her? Charlotte wondered an hour later as she drove home in her loaned Volvo. Was this stupid infatuation she seemed to have developed for Oliver Tennant nature's way of rebelling against the cautious, defensive way she lived her life? She hoped so . . . just as she hoped that these dangerous and unwelcome feelings of hers would fade quickly and quietly once they were confronted with the reality of sharing her home with him. There was nothing like a touch of realism for destroying idealistic daydreams, she told herself firmly as she turned into her drive.

The sun had gone in; the overgrown rhododendrons cast dark shadows over the drive, turning it into a secret, almost brooding place, so that she shivered momentarily, and then derided herself. She was letting Sheila's mother-henning get to her. She had driven up and down this drive a thousand times without even giving it a second thought...

The workmen were on the point of leaving as she arrived, the chaos in the kitchen making her gulp and bravely swallow the dismayed words springing to her lips. Was it really possible for the pretty, warm kitchen she had visualised from the drawings Mr Burns had done for her to actually materialise from this mess of plaster, wood, exposed wires and heaven alone knew what else?

'We've managed to turn the electricity back on for you,' Mr Burns told her. 'And your cooker's fixed up in the pantry, like you asked. Seems like we're going to have a problem with the plumbing, though. Lead pipes,' he added succinctly, as though that explained everything.

Charlotte blinked and waited for enlightenment.

'Not safe...not these days,' he told her warningly. 'They'll have to be replaced.'

In her mind's eye, Charlotte saw another nought being added to his original estimate and suppressed a faint sigh. 'How long do you think it will be before you're finished?' she asked him fatalistically.

'Well, provided we don't come up with any more set-backs...should be all done middle of next week or so.'

Smiling weakly, Charlotte stepped over what she guessed were her old kitchen units and what now looked like a pile of firewood, and headed for the door into the hallway.

Mrs Higham should have been today. To Charlotte's surprise she had been quite approving when Charlotte informed her about Oliver. Mrs Higham sometimes had a rather unconventional attitude towards her work, preferring to choose for herself which tasks she would and would not do, rather than be directed, and because Charlotte knew how difficult it would be to replace her she had put up with her eccentricities. She had already asked her to clean through the rooms which were going to be Oliver's and make up the bed, but it might be as well to check that she had.

Charlotte heard the workmen driving away as she opened the room into the bedroom which her father had used as his study. The window was open, allowing the newly rehung curtains to move gently in the breeze. Her father's old desk stood under the window to catch the best of the light. The house still retained its original bedroom fireplaces, thanks to her father's refusal to entertain any modernisation, and Charlotte saw with a small start of surprise that Mrs Higham had left a fire laid in the grate, and filled a basket of logs.

Oliver was certainly getting star treatment, she acknowledged wryly as she saw the trouble the cleaner had gone to. She had certainly never left a fire laid in *her* bedroom, Charlotte reflected as she opened the door into the bedroom.

The bedroom still contained the heavy dark furniture that had originally belonged to her grandparents. Her father had never seen the necessity of replacing the cumbersome wardrobes with something more modern, even fitted. The darkness of the furniture, combined with the dark green carpet, gave the room an austere male aura, Charlotte thought, a frown furrowing her forehead as she moved towards the bed and saw that it wasn't made up.

That meant that *she* would have to do it. Her father had not been a mean man precisely, but he had always hated waste, which was why Charlotte was still using the heavy linen sheets which again had come from her grandparents' home. Since it was impossible to launder these at home in the way her father insisted upon, a weekly laundry service collected and delivered these items, and Charlotte prayed that she would find sufficient clean and aired linen in the airing cupboard to make up the bed.

It was her own fault, of course; she should have checked on these things instead of leaving it to Mrs Higham.

To her relief she found what she wanted in the airing cupboard. Carrying the sheets and bedding through into the bedroom, she put them down on the bed. Before she did anything else, she would make herself something to eat and have a cup of coffee. That was, if she could find the coffee.

It was impossible for her to eat in the kitchen, of course, and so she took her omelette and coffee through into the small sitting-room on the side of the house. From here she could look out into the back garden with its tangle of overgrown lawns and flowerbeds.

It had rained just after she had come in, a short, heavy shower, and now the late spring flowers drooped sadly under the weight of the raindrops. On impulse, after she had finished her meal, she opened the french windows and stepped outside. Half an hour later, her arms full of flowers she had had no intention of picking, she went into the pantry and deftly arranged them in two large jugs. She left one jug in the sitting-room, and took the other upstairs with her.

Until she had actually set it down on the polished desk, she had had no idea why she had picked the flowers, and now, standing back from the bright warmth of them, she felt her skin burn with self-knowledge. She was just about to snatch the jug back and remove it when she heard Oliver's car.

The bed still wasn't made, and, ignoring the flowers, she went quickly into the bedroom, hurriedly covering the bed in the crisp linen sheets.

She heard the car stop just as she finished, and, giving the rooms one last assessing glance, she hurried downstairs to welcome her new lodger.

'I'll take you upstairs,' she told him as she opened the door to him, wondering if he would register her nervousness and guess at the cause of it, and then telling herself not to be so stupid. The way she was acting, she was practically begging him to guess how she felt. 'Then I'll leave you to get settled in, if you've got an early start in the morning.'

They were halfway upstairs, and she paused and added uncertainly, wondering if he would expect a meal, 'The kitchen is in chaos. I'm using the pantry to cook in.'

'It's all right. I ate before I left the Bull.'

Charlotte opened the door to the study and walked in, waiting for Oliver to follow her. She saw the way he looked at the made-up fire and from it to the flowers on the desk.

'It all looks very welcoming,' he told her softly, walking over to the desk. 'I don't think I've enjoyed having garden flowers in my room since I left home. There's something very evocative of a real home about garden-cut flowers rather than bought ones, don't you think?'

'Mrs Higham put them there,' Charlotte lied, wishing she could do something about the frantic race of her heart. When he reached out and touched one of the tell-tale wet petals of one flower, she was glad he wasn't looking at her to see the rich tide of colour burning her skin.

'I'll leave you to get settled in,' she reiterated, and then fled to the door before she could make even more of a fool of herself.

Why on earth had she lied to him like that? It would have been simple enough to say that she had brought the flowers in to save them being battered by further rain, but no...she had had to go and behave like a love-crazed adolescent.

For a moment, making up the bed, she had actually lifted one of the linen-covered pillows to her face, imagining how it would feel against her skin if it carried his scent. The sharp twisting sensation that had coiled through her stomach had alerted her to what she was doing...what she was thinking. She hadn't thought about a man in such sexually explicit terms since...since she had left

her teenage years behind; and it shamed her now
that her body should react so swiftly and so wantonly to the mental image of Oliver's naked body.

While Oliver made several journeys up and down
the stairs with his possessions, Charlotte worked
diligently on some paperwork she had brought
home with her, determined to keep out of his way
and not to embarrass either herself or him by trying
to put their relationship on anything other than a
business footing.

When he had finished, he rapped briefly on the
sitting-room door and then came in.

'That's finished. I was wondering if you'd like
to go out for a drink somewhere . . . to celebrate our
joint appointment this afternoon.'

Charlotte felt her heart leap, but almost immediately she shook her head. 'No, thank you,' she told
him dampeningly.

He was just being polite, she told herself, trying
to ignore the possibility of a more sinister purpose
in his invitation. She was almost sure that Vanessa
was wrong . . . almost sure. His offer of a drink was
simply a polite gesture, which she was pretty sure
he expected her to refuse.

Certainly he didn't *look* particularly disap-
pointed when she did.

'Well, perhaps another time,' was all he said, and
then he cheerfully excused himself, going back upstairs, leaving her to wish that she weren't the sort
of person she was and that she had the kind of self-
confidence so evident in women like Vanessa. That
she was the kind of woman who knew that no man

would ever ask her out simply out of compassion or good manners, but because he was attracted to her and found her desirable.

The thought of Oliver finding her desirable sent such a charge of sensation through her that her body tensed against it. How was it possible for him to make her feel like this? Desire...it was something she had comfortably assumed would never dominate her life. She had thought that, if she didn't inspire sensual need in men, than at least she had the advantage of being free from experiencing it herself, but now she was discovering that all her comfortable and safe beliefs about herself were being swept aside...that she could indeed experience desire, and that it was a sharp, raking, painful sensation which made her body ache restlessly and her mind fill with such wanton mental images that she could feel the heat they generated crawling up under her skin.

It was a relief when she was finally able to go to bed, but sleep didn't come easily. She was far too conscious of Oliver sleeping so close to her.

So close physically, maybe, but so very far away emotionally and mentally.

She had to get a grip on herself before it was too late, she warned herself. But too late for what? She wasn't merely in love with Oliver Tennant—she loved him, which was infinitely worse. She sat bolt upright in bed as the truth burst upon her—irrefutable and inescapable. She loved him!

CHAPTER EIGHT

THE moment she opened her eyes, Charlotte was aware of a heavy sense of despair. Outside her bedroom window the sun was shining, but inside her heart everything was shadowed and dulled by the pain of knowing that she loved Oliver.

Oliver... Instinctively she glanced at her bedside clock. The house was silent, so presumably he had already left. It was extraordinary that, even knowing the folly of her emotions, even knowing that she was safer when he was absent, that every second spent in his company increased the intensity of her feelings, and the danger that she might somehow betray them, she should still feel this total sense of desolation in the knowledge that he wasn't there.

She shivered under the bedclothes, not because she was cold, but because of the feelings prickling her skin.

God knew, she didn't want to feel like this—had never imagined she *could* feel like this—and, if anyone other than herself should discover what she *did* feel, she thought she would die from the humiliation of it.

Restlessly she pushed back the bedclothes and got up. Her father's old rooms had their own bathroom which had been installed when he had become too ill to walk very far.

Her bathroom was a couple of doors down the corridor; knowing she had the house to herself, she didn't hesitate to open her bedroom door and walk on to the landing wearing the faded soft cotton pyjama jacket which was her preferred nightwear. She had several of them, all of them washed to a similar state of faded softness. Frilly nightdresses were not for her, and when she had returned from London she had eschewed the chain-store-bought nightshirts she had worn then in favour of the discarded top halves of pyjamas she suspected had originally belonged to her father, and which she had found abandoned in one of the house's many chests of drawers.

Now, absently noticing how thin the cotton was wearing, she acknowledged ruefully that she would soon have to replace them, but with what? She had grown accustomed to the softness of a quality of cotton no longer cheaply available.

Automatically, having walked out on to the landing, she followed her normal routine of making her way downstairs to make some coffee. This was her morning ritual, to make the freshly brewed coffee she enjoyed so much, despite its heavy caffeine content, and then go upstairs to shower and dress so that the fragrant brew was waiting for her when she came back down.

The kitchen floor felt cold beneath her bare feet, her toes curling instinctively at the chilly contact. Beyond the kitchen window, she could see the dew-dampened outline of the lawns and flowerbeds, softened into mystical beauty by their covering of moisture. She paused for a moment to admire the miracle of nature, admitting how much she would miss these simple pleasures of living in the country-side if she were ever forced to return to city living.

Grimacing a little at the state of the kitchen, she hurried into the pantry, and started to fill the filter machine's jug with cold water. It was while she was doing so, her back to the door, that she felt the unmistakable chilliness of cold fresh air, as though a door had been opened.

Immediately she tensed, swinging round, her eyes rounding in dismayed shock as she saw Oliver standing in the open doorway. Unlike her, he was fully dressed in an immaculate business suit and a crisp white shirt.

'I thought you'd gone.'

The words left her throat in a husky whisper that sounded more like an apology than the accusation she had intended it to be.

'I'm just on my way. Unfortunately I couldn't resist walking round the garden before I left.' He grimaced as he looked down at his very wet shoes. 'I'd forgotten how wet dew can be. I was just on my way upstairs to change my shoes when I heard you in here.'

'I came down to put the coffee on,' Charlotte told him awkwardly, suddenly conscious of how she must look, her hair uncombed, her face unwashed, dressed in an oversized and worn pyjama jacket that was surely the opposite kind of nightwear someone like Vanessa would choose to sleep in.

She stepped forward awkwardly and stopped, blinking in the full beam of the sunlight shining in through the window to momentarily blind her. She heard Oliver catch his breath, almost as though in shock, and her own nerve-endings responded automatically to the sound so that she froze where she was.

'I'd better go and change these shoes,' she heard him saying in a harsh, rasping voice that for some reason made her throat ache.

She wanted him to take her in his arms, to hold her, to kiss her. Angry with herself, she blinked in the strong light, and watched the movements of his tall, lithe body, wondering bleakly at the unfairness of nature. Why couldn't it have been content with simply giving him his overpowering physical maleness? Why had it had to add the kind of personality she felt so in tune with that she was helpless to defend herself against the impact of his emotional and physical effect on her.

She heard him go upstairs, and stayed where she was until she heard him come down again to leave via the front door, bleakly wondering why it hurt so much that he hadn't come back into the pantry to say goodbye to her.

Ten minutes later, when she walked into her bathroom, she thought she knew the answer, or at least part of it, and her face turned deep pink with embarrassment. Sunshine flooded her bathroom as it had done in the pantry, but here in the bathroom she had the advantage of seeing in the mirrors that lined its walls the effect that sunlight had.

The soft cotton of her pyjama jacket, so warm and bulky to her touch, had turned virtually transparent in the strong sunshine, so that when she stood bathed in its light the entire shape of her body,

every one of its contours and curves, could be seen
quite clearly delineated beneath the jacket, right
down to the soft shadowing between her thighs and
the deep rose areola of her breasts.

From being flushed her skin drained of colour
as she stared in mortification at her own reflection.
This was what Oliver had seen when he'd walked
into the pantry. No wonder he had left so quickly.

He must have thought...what? That she had
come downstairs deliberately knowing that he was
there, wanting him to see her like that. Had that
been what he'd thought? Did he think she had
actually...?

Her heart was beating far too fast, a nauseous
churning feeling burning her empty stomach. She
started to tremble. Why on earth hadn't she checked
before going downstairs? Why hadn't she realised
he was still there? But it was too late now for such
recriminations. The damage was done.

All day long it was on her mind, a poison eating
into her, so that several times Sheila watched her
worriedly, wondering what was wrong.

'Aren't you feeling very well?' she asked at one
point, causing Charlotte to lift her head from her
paperwork.

'I'm fine. Why?' she asked defensively.

Sheila shrugged. 'Well, it's just that it's such a
beautiful day, and you're all wrapped up in that
thick woollen sweater.'

Sheila herself was wearing a very pretty short-
sleeved blouse which showed off her feminine
figure, and Charlotte, who with that incident in the

pantry very much to the forefront of her mind had deliberately dressed in the most body-muffling clothes she could find, felt her face burn with guilt and humiliation.

In actual fact she felt almost stifled in the sweater, which was more appropriate for cold mid-winter wear than a soft late spring day, but, with her mind still full of mental visions of how she had looked this morning, she had writhed in mental torment and deliberately wrapped herself in as many muffling layers of clothing as she could endure.

'I . . . I didn't realise how warm it was going to be,' she mumbled, knowing that she was flushing and hoping that Sheila would put her high colour down to the warmth of her unseasonal clothes.

During the afternoon, Charlotte took Sophy with her when she drove out to Hadley Court to measure up the house and to start taking details of those items of furniture which were going to be auctioned.

Sophy proved very quick to follow her directions, and by the end of the afternoon Charlotte was ready to acknowledge that, in doing the younger girl a favour by giving her a job, she had probably done herself one as well, providing always that Oliver left her with enough business to merit employing both Sheila and Sophy.

Oliver had indicated repeatedly that he didn't want to put her out of business, that he believed the area was large enough to provide sufficient business for both of them. There was something about him, some intrinsic basic honesty that compelled her to believe he meant what he was saying, but was he right? Only time would tell.

But if they both stayed in the area, how was she going to cope with her feelings? Already it was getting harder to conceal them, and, although she knew it was the best possible thing for her, she was dreading the time coming when he would move out of her home and into his own.

Common sense told her that her best course of action would be to put as much distance between them as possible. Perhaps if she didn't have the business and Sheila and Sophy to consider, she might consider selling up and...

Who was she trying to deceive? she asked herself tiredly as she dropped Sophy off at home and then drove back to the office. She had no intention of doing any such thing. Her brain might tell her one thing, but her heart was telling her something entirely different.

She wanted to be close to him. She wanted to be where he was, self-destructive though she knew such a desire was.

She was a fool, she berated herself tiredly at half-past six when she finally locked up the office and went out to her loaned car. If she had any sense...but what woman in love ever exhibited that particular virtue?

Halfway home, tired and hot, she pulled off the road and crossly removed her bulky sweater. She was aching to get home and shower the sticky heat of the day off her body. The fine wool shirt she was wearing beneath the sweater was clinging uncomfortably to her skin, and, as she wound down the windows and restarted the car, she pushed her fingers into her hair, savouring the cooling effect of the light breeze on her hot, tense scalp.

Oliver's car was parked outside the house, a reminder of his generosity in offering to lend it to her. She had been wrong about him in so many ways; it was tempting to allow herself to daydream that she might be wrong in others... that the occasional, disturbing glint of sensual awareness she had surprised in his eyes when he looked at her might actually mean something... that that kiss he had given her, the words he had said to her, could have sprung from something other than pity.

Telling herself not to be such a fool, she stopped the car and got out.

The workmen had left for the day, and as she walked round to the back door she found herself hoping that she would not find the same chaos in her kitchen she had discovered the previous evening. The door was open, making her stop and frown over the carelessness of the workmen.

While she was still staring at the open door, she suddenly heard Oliver saying cheerfully behind her, 'Ah, good, it is you. I thought it must be.'

She turned round to be confronted by the unexpected sight of his naked torso, tanned still with a faint golden residue of the previous summer's sun, the dark hair that was such a disturbingly visual reminder of his masculinity damp with sweat.

As she stared at him, he pushed a grimy hand through his already ruffled hair, leaving a streak of dirt on his forehead and making her stomach muscles clench against the wave of sensuality and

desire that rose up inside her at the sight and scent
of his sun-warmed body.

'I got back earlier than I expected, so I thought
I'd make good use of the weather and make a start
on the garden,' he was saying cheerfully, adding
more cautiously, 'You did say you didn't mind.'

Didn't mind... what was it she wasn't supposed
to mind? she wondered dazedly. The sight of his
half-naked body, clad in a pair of faded ancient
jeans that seemed to cling lovingly to the lean length
of his legs, outlining the powerful muscles of his
thighs, the scent of his body, warm,
musky... male... was so powerfully arousing that
she wanted to walk blindly towards him, to breathe
in that musky aphrodisiac maleness, to explore the
powerful muscles of his shoulders and torso with
her hands and her lips.

She started to tremble, a deep-rooted, aching
physical reaction to the sight of him. She wanted
to walk up to him and to slide her hands against
the taut flesh above the waistband of his jeans, to
unfasten them and to discover if that tormenting
line of damp, dark hair...

A shocked moan of self-contempt broke the
silence between them; her eyes were wild with panic
as she tried to focus on the garden beyond him, to
strive for some measure of normality and sanity in
a world that suddenly seemed to have turned completely upside-down.

It was men who were supposed to feel this intense sexual need, wasn't it? Not women... at least,
not when nothing had been said or done to encourage it.

Beneath the thick covering of her blouse she could feel her nipples hardening, aching. And, as her breath caught in her throat, she suffered the humiliation of the unbearably erotic mental image of herself, free of the cumbersome burden of her clothes, her body pressed close to Oliver's, so that the tormented pulse of her swollen breasts was eased by the physical contact of their bodies, so that her paler, feminine flesh was rubbed erotically by the darker, harder maleness of his.

'Charlotte.'

An anxiety in his voice brought her sharply back to reality. As his hand reached out towards her, she stepped back from him, such a look of revulsion in her eyes that he frowned, not realising that it was directed against herself.

'I'm sorry... I'd forgotten. I must be filthy. It's just that for a moment you looked...'

Charlotte turned her back on him. She didn't want him to tell her how she had looked. She felt sick and faint, stripped of her defences, struggling to come to terms with a latent sensuality she had never dreamed she possessed.

'I expect you'll be eating out tonight,' she said awkwardly. 'I...'

'Well, as a matter of fact, I had thought we might eat together.'

His words stopped her, so that she had turned round to face him again before she knew what she was doing, her face registering her shock.

'Together? But——'

'It's by way of a small celebration. I've sold my London agency for an excellent price, and I was hoping that you might be kind enough to help me to celebrate my decision to make my home permanently down here.'

'Me? But——'

'Please...I've brought a special Fortnum's hamper back with me so that we wouldn't need to cook.'

Charlotte was staring at him. She couldn't take in what he was saying. 'You want to celebrate with me,' she repeated jerkily. 'But...'

'But what?'

How on earth had he come to be standing so close to her? She blinked dizzily, wondering when he had closed the distance between them.

He was so close to her now that if she gave in to the temptation to close her eyes and sway close to him her hair would brush that bare, moist chest, and then if she turned her head her lips would touch the satin smoothness of his throat. And, if she did, he would only have to close his hands on her shoulders to bring her body into intimate contact with his and to relieve the aching tension tormenting her.

'But what?' he repeated softly, causing her to focus on him and then step back from him, her eyes shadowed and wary.

But why me? she wanted to ask, but dared not. Instead she said as coolly as she could, 'I should have thought you would have friends in London you could have celebrated with.'

'Not friends,' he corrected her. 'Acquaintances, yes. London is that kind of place. Everyone is too busy carving a career for themselves these days to have time to establish friendships. That kind of lifestyle isn't for me any longer. Mature, sensible relationships where two individuals agree to spend a tiny portion of their time together, sharing their bodies without sharing their dreams...that's not for me.'

She was starting to tremble wildly, unable to allow herself to believe what she was hearing.

'You mean you want...friendship...from me?' She trembled uncertainly over the word friendship, not sure of anything any more, feeling as though she had strayed into an unfamiliar world where there were no markers for her to follow.

She saw the way his mouth twisted and felt sharp anxiety spear her. She had angered him in some way.

'Is that so very hard to understand?' he asked her quietly.

'I——'

'Look, I'm filthy and sweaty. Let me go and shower, and then we can talk over dinner. You won't have to do a thing. In fact, if you like we could eat outside.'

'Outside?' Charlotte stared at him.

'Mmm. It's going to be a lovely warm evening.'

Eat outside... How long had it been since she had done anything like that? Not even when she had been a child had her father believed in the spontaneity of picnics and eating outdoors. Her childhood, she had come to recognise, had been very regimented. A certain code of behaviour had been imposed on her and rigidly adhered to.

'I think there are some deck-chairs in the shed,' she began uncertainly. 'But——'

Oliver shook his head. 'Leave everything to me. Give me half an hour.'

Half an hour...

Now she had five minutes of that half-hour left, Charlotte saw, as she stood in front of her bedroom mirror and stared at her reflection.

What did one wear for an al-fresco meal in the garden with a man who wanted one as a friend? She had no idea, having no previous experience of such a thing, and in the end, after she had showered, washed and dried her hair and replaced her make-up, she had dressed uncertainly in a pair of jeans nearly as old and snug-fitting as Oliver's had been, although hers were clean, and a long-sleeved, soft pink top in T-shirt fabric, which had a pretty scooped neckline and a row of buttons down the front.

She had chosen the top because it was light and cool without being in any way brief or revealing. Only, as she went downstairs to join Oliver in the kitchen, she realised that she had not allowed for the intensity of his effect on her body, and she prayed that the now familiar tightening of her nipples was not visible to him through the fabric of her top.

Like her, he was wearing jeans—clean ones—and a soft cotton shirt, unbuttoned at the throat, with the sleeves rolled back to reveal the warm strength of his forearms.

A wicker hamper stood on the kitchen table and with it was an ice bucket complete with champagne and two glasses. Her eyes widened as she looked at it, an unfamiliar warm sense of pleasure igniting inside her as she realised that he must have been thinking of this...of her...while he was in London.

Or was she reading too much into what he had said? She darted him an uncertain glance, and was immediately reassured by the warmth of his smile, almost as though he knew what she was thinking...what she was feeling. But that was impossible, of course; there was no way he could know. He was just being pleasant. He was lonely, and wanted her company.

'Chairs,' she began vaguely, trying to concentrate her mind on something mundane.

'All organised. If you could carry the champagne, I'll bring the hamper.'

As they walked out into the garden, still warm, as he had forecast, still bathed in sunshine, he started to tell her about the sale of his business, and of the visit he had managed to make to a friend who worked for one of the London agents who specialised in dealing with large houses and country estates.

'It seems they may have a buyer for Hadley Court,' he told her as he guided her down the path that ran alongside the lawn. 'He's going to get in touch with us later in the week when he's made contact with his client. I've given him your number as well as mine. His client is a private buyer, wanting a property for his own occupation.'

'Oh, that's marvellous!'

It was impossible to conceal her relief. She stopped on the path and turned towards him, her eyes shining, her face turned up to his, and then she tensed as she saw his expression change.

Her mouth had gone oddly dry; she could hear the shallow rapidity of her own heartbeat. An odd lazy heat seemed to be engulfing her.

He's going to kiss me, she thought dizzily... but then, just as she was about to step closer to him, he moved back, so that she had no option but to follow him along the path. Hot colour flooded her as he backed off from her and moved away.

'Where are we going?' she asked him, striving to appear unconcerned and relaxed, praying he hadn't realised she had thought he was going to kiss her.

'Here,' he told her, gesturing towards the small orchard tucked away at the bottom of the garden.

The soft grass beneath the trees was thick with fallen blossom, the evening air heavy with its scent. Under the largest of the trees was a rug heaped with cushions. The setting was idyllic, like something out of a painting... a scene set for seduction.

Seduction? Did Oliver intend to seduce her? The sheer unexpectedness of what her senses were telling her shimmered through her, creating a warm welling of delighted shock, so that bubbles of disbelieving amusement combined with a heady sense of having strayed into a magical world of fantasy whirled into her bloodstream, making her buoyant and light-headed.

Like her, he had stopped walking, and now they faced one another. How did one ask a man if he was merely trying to provide a comfortable setting for a shared meal or whether it was something more intimate that he had in mind? And why would Oliver want to make love to her? Her face burned suddenly as she remembered how he had seen her this morning.

Did he think this was what she wanted? Had he gone to all this trouble simply because he felt sorry for her? Did men make love to women they felt sorry for?

Suddenly very deflated and miserable, she said uncomfortably, 'Oliver, I——'

'I'm hungry,' he interrupted her firmly. 'Let's eat, and then we can talk.'

He sounded so matter-of-fact and calm that it seemed idiotic that she should have thought even for a split second that he might have intended to make love to her, and so she followed him into the orchard and allowed him to settle her comfortably against the cushions, while he opened the hamper and removed its contents.

Charlotte blinked in astonishment at the luxury of the food inside. No sandwiches here, but instead tiny delicate quiches filled with salmon and other delicacies, so mouth-wateringly delicious that they were impossible to resist.

The champagne, cool and refreshing, bubbled in her glass.

And, as Oliver drank his own, he said softly, 'This is how champagne should be drunk: in a warm garden filled with the scents of summer, with a beautiful woman by your side.'

Charlotte started to tremble. She gulped at her champagne to hide her agitation, and said quickly,

'I can't believe this food is for a picnic. It's so luxurious.'

There was fresh salmon and an appetising collection of salad and vegetables, crusty French bread, strawberries and thick cream, all served on china with silver cutlery, and a beautifully starched tablecloth and napkins.

Luxury indeed.

'It's the kind of hamper they do for events such as Glyndebourne,' Oliver told her.

When had his eyes narrowed to that sharp, almost glinting intensity that seemed to see through the defences she was trying to put up against him?

'More champagne?'

She stared at him, and then realised that her glass was empty. She let him fill it, and drank it quickly while he watched her with unnerving intensity.

Despite the deliciousness of the food, she could barely touch it; she was too tense, too on edge. The champagne, though, was a different thing. She drank three full glasses and felt its mellow, uninhibiting effect on her body. She couldn't stand the tension any longer.

Recklessly she turned to Oliver and asked huskily, 'Oliver, are you going to make love to me?'

For a moment he was silent, and then he asked in turn, 'Is that what you want me to do?'

It wasn't the answer she had wanted. She bit her lip and stared at him, her mind suddenly fogged and confused by the champagne, her body and its desires, ignoring the cautioning whispers of her brain, challenging her to say fiercely, 'Yes. Yes, I do.'

Oliver was so still that she thought she must have shocked him, but it was too late to retract now, too late to wonder dizzily why she had behaved in such an outrageous fashion, and to wonder even more why she should feel so unconcerned about it. She had never experienced before this extraordinary sense of being so cut free from her normal anxieties and self-doubts—perhaps because she was not normally in the habit of drinking so much strong champagne on an empty stomach.

'I've been thinking about this all day,' she heard Oliver saying thickly as he drew her towards him, his hands stroking the fragile bones of her shoulders, and then moving up to slide into her hair and tilt her head, so that she couldn't have avoided the descent of his head even if she had wanted to.

He tasted of champagne, she recognised absently, as his mouth met hers—not as it had done before, in an explorative, gentle kiss, but open and moist, so that her heart leapt in heady response to the tension within him, and her body rejoiced in the sheer pleasure of knowing she aroused his desire.

While he kissed her, his hands shaped the back of her head, then her back itself, right down to her waist and beyond until they were cupping her bottom and pulling her into his body.

Now her earlier fantasy took on the shape of reality. It was true that her top and his shirt were between them, but she could still feel the rapid thud of his heart against her body, and her stomach clenched on the sensation of her breasts pushing against his chest, wanting a more intimate contact with his flesh.

As he kissed her, odd, tormented mental images flashed through her brain, and when he slid his mouth from hers to her throat she said huskily, 'This morning...I didn't...'

The champagne still clouded her mind, still relaxed her inhibitions and cautions.

'I did,' Oliver told her groaningly, his mouth against her ear, sending fierce shivers of pleasure over her skin. 'I looked at you in that damned pyjama top and the last thing I wanted to do was to leave you and go to London.'

The new Charlotte, the one she had never known existed before, the one who seemed recklessly to court ever-increasing danger, whispered coaxingly, 'What did you want to do?'

At the sound of the words a mild shock ran through her, but there was also a sense of accomplishment, of pleasure almost in what she had done as she felt Oliver's body tense for a moment before he whispered rawly, 'I wanted to take you back upstairs to bed, and unfasten those damned buttons, one by one, like this...'

Like what? She was lost in the dreamy warmth of delight conjured up by his words, and it was several seconds before she realised that he actually was unfastening the buttons on her top, and that his lean dark hand really was lying against the exposed upper curve of her breast, that his gaze had actually found the small dark mole just hidden under the edge of her bra, and that his mouth had left her ear and was now nibbling its way along her throat, and down over her collarbone to the place where he had pushed aside the fine cotton of her bra, so that his tongue could touch that small dark dot of flesh.

Why should such a light, delicate physical contact release such a flood of heat inside her? she wondered muzzily. Why should the pressure of his hand against her breast make her want to moan and tear away the cloth barriers between it and the bareness of her skin? Why should it make her want to turn to him and press her mouth against his throat, her body against his, to...?

'And then I'd have done this,' she heard Oliver saying silkily against her skin, his voice so soft and gentle it seemed to lap over her in warm waves, making her sink deeper and deeper into the delicious sea of sensuality in which she was floating.

She felt his hands removing her bra and sighed voluptuously in pleasure as they touched her skin; she felt his mouth moving against her breast and moved eagerly to speed it on its journey to the summit of her nipple. The sensation of his mouth bathing the aching pulse of her flesh in moist heat made her spine arch and a soft moan of pleasure leave her throat.

After that, for a long time, the only sounds disturbing the peace of the evening were the soft ones of pleasure Charlotte smothered against Oliver's skin as mindlessly she gave in to the urgings of her body and put into practice the fantasies she had indulged in earlier. The sensation of Oliver's hands and mouth against her own flesh, as he slowly revealed inch after inch of her body between whispered words of such promise that her body melted, was slowly driving her out of control. There was no one in the whole world but Oliver...nothing in the universe but the intimacy they were sharing.

She heard him groan when her hands stroked the flat plane of his belly, felt the sound reverberate against her mouth as she caressed his throat, and then cried out in aching pleasure herself when his hand touched her intimately and her body opened out to him, so femininely enticing and arousing that he whispered things against her skin which turned her mindless with delight. A delight that was doubled when she realised that he shared her need, her desire. It was surely impossible that *she* could arouse him to this pitch of intensity, this fierce, pulsing desire that he told her raggedly he no longer had the power to check. This could not be reality.

Once he hesitated, almost as though he was asking her...what? For permission to possess her? Hadn't she already given that permission without words...with the sensual pleading of her flesh when it so wantonly invited his touch?

Soon they would be lovers. Lovers... She shivered in expectant anticipation, wanting him, aching for him, knowing recklessly that whatever might follow she would always have this...always have the knowledge that he had desired her.

Deep down inside her a small voice struggled to be heard, to warn her that something was wrong, that this physical intimacy was too much, too soon, that there were things which should have been said, but it was drowned out, deafened by the fierce sensation of need that pierced her when Oliver drew her down on the rug beneath him, covering her body with his, fitting himself against her as her body, more knowing than she had dreamed, moved to accommodate the weight and heat of him.

Her heart was racing frantically, all her senses concentrating on the pleasure that lured her on.

The brief cessation of his hands and mouth caressing her skin, drugging her senses with delight upon delight, promise upon promise, confused her, so that when his hands shaped her face and she looked into his eyes she felt a momentary schism within her, a sudden stabbing realisation of what she was doing, but then she felt Oliver's mouth move against her own and heard him saying rawly, 'My God, I shouldn't be doing this, but it's too late now to stop.'

The pressure of his lips on hers hardened, quickening her pulses, his tongue plunging fiercely into the moist sweetness of her mouth, the movements of his body against hers relentlessly driving them both to a pitch of such intense desire that she cried out in tormented frustration as she waited impatiently for the first thrust of his body within her own, welcoming it with such voluptuous pleasure that he cried out in turn, abandoning himself to the enticement of her, taking them both so far beyond the boundaries of earthly reality that Charlotte felt briefly she had become immortal, capable of touching the stars in their heavens, capable of reaching to every part of the universe, and most of all capable of giving this man who was holding her, and whom she was holding in turn, such pleasure and fulfilment that the rest of their lives would become as irreversibly entwined as their bodies.

The pleasure, once so sharp and piercing, so unbelievably immense, died slowly, floating her back down to earth, to the realisation that she was lying naked in Oliver's arms, on a rug under the shade of one of her own apple trees...that odd blossoms had drifted down from the tree and now lay against Oliver's skin.

She touched them gently, too deliciously inert to even think of moving, her body so unbelievably relaxed and lazy that she wanted to stretch like a cat with the pleasure of being inside her own skin.

The thought made her smile. Oliver reached out and touched her mouth with his fingertip.

'Why didn't you tell me?' he asked her softly.

She flushed defensively, distracted by the subtle sensation of pleasure evoked by the teasing movement of his finger, and then said honestly, 'It never occurred to me. Did you mind...that I hadn't...?'

'Had another lover.' He shook his head, but already she could sense a constraint in him that was communicating itself to her.

Like Eve in the garden of Eden, she was abruptly conscious of her nudity, of what she had done and why, but the euphoria of the pleasure they had shared still warmed her veins, and it was easy to dismiss the vague doubts crowding the edge of her mind like the shadows stealing over the garden when she bit softly at the tormenting finger and watched desire banish the constraint from Oliver's eyes, saw and felt the immediate response of his body to her own as she moved softly against him.

This time, it was different; this time he took her deeper into an intimacy she had never suspected she would experience, never mind enjoy.

She discovered why the dark arrowing of hair disappearing beneath the waistband of his jeans had tormented her senses so, and how powerful and feminine it made her feel when her own longing drove her to caress him intimately, to place her mouth against him and to feel his instant uncontrollable response.

The things he said to her, the way he touched her, these were things she would treasure until the end of her days, she acknowledged tiredly, nestling close to him a little later.

At first she had been hurt, had ached both emotionally and physically, when he had refused the mute invitation of her body to possess it a second time, but when he had gently explained to her that he didn't want to hurt her, that there were other ways he could ease the tension she was suffering, that giving her pleasure gave it back to him, she had allowed him to show her what he had meant, a little shocked by the intimacy of his mouth against the inner core of her body until the pleasure that racked her overwhelmed everything but the need to accede to its demands.

Now, she felt boneless, and only one cloud dimmed the haze of pleasure bathing her. It worried at the corner of her mind, keeping just out of reach so that she couldn't quite grasp it. Something that hadn't been said...something wrong...but she was asleep before she could grasp what it was.

As she slipped into sleep Oliver studied her wryly. Things had got dangerously out of hand. All he had intended had been a little light lovemaking, a breaking down of the boundaries between them as a prelude to the relationship he wanted to have with her—a slow, gentle courtship.

That abrupt question she had asked him, demanding to know if he wanted to make love to her, had taken them both way, way beyond what he had intended. His body rejoiced in what they had shared, in the way she had responded to him, but his mind...

He sighed faintly, knowing that, in giving in to the desire that had been burning in him ever since he first met her, he had probably caused himself more problems than he had solved.

Why, when, after all the years of being alone and being content to be alone, he did meet the woman he loved, should she be this stubborn, defensive creature, who refused to believe just how very desirable a man might find her? Any man... not just himself.

He smiled mirthlessly to himself. Part of him wanted to open her eyes to reality, to show her that it was her own attitude that prevented his sex from making overtures towards her, not any innate lack of desirability; another part of him selfishly wanted to keep that knowledge from her, so that he could never lose her to someone else.

Brushing a small spider off her sleeping face, he wondered how long it would be before she realised the potential consequences of what they had done.

Unprotected sex... the very first rule that should have governed the kind of intimacy they had just shared had been ignored by both of them.

He found himself dangerously hoping that he might have made her pregnant. That way...

Fool, he chided himself, standing up, and then bending to lift her into his arms.

The evening breeze cooled his flesh, and he grinned to himself as he contemplated the picture they must make, both of them mother-naked, she in his arms, her body still bearing the faint betraying signs of his lovemaking...of his possession.

Something hot and primitive stirred in his stomach—a male possessiveness he hadn't realised until now he could feel. She was his now...

As he carried her into the house and upstairs, she stirred in her sleep, turning her head to nestle her face into his shoulder, her hand pressing against his chest; he wondered if he dared put her in his own bed. He wanted the pleasure of waking up beside her in the morning, the certainty of knowing...

But no, things were going to be difficult enough as it was. Ruefully he carried her into her own room, slipping her beneath the covers, before going back outside to retrieve their clothes and to clear away the remains of their picnic. As he picked up the empty champagne bottle, he grimaced to himself. It had not been his intention to make her tipsy. She had been the one to insist on having her glass refilled.

Was he fool to hope that, because she desired him, she must also love him as he loved her?

Tomorrow would tell. He wished he had had the courage to tell her how he felt as they made love, but he had been terrified that if he did she would withdraw from him, and honesty compelled him to admit that in the urgency of his own arousal his physical desire had momentarily been stronger than his emotional need to tell her what he felt for her.

He had plucked himself a very thorny rose indeed, he reflected, as he headed back to the house. Perhaps a romantic breakfast, a room full of red roses... And then he remembered that the workmen were all too likely to arrive even before she had woken up, and he abandoned such a scheme.

CHAPTER NINE

CHARLOTTE overslept. Waking up was like clawing her way through sticky treacle, interspersed every now and again by sharp fragments of memory that lacerated and bruised her, so that by the time she eventually got her eyes open her skin was hot with the shocked acid self-disgust gnawing at her stomach.

How *could* she have done what she did? How could she have got drunk and then begged Oliver to make love to her? And not just once but...

Moaning, she rolled over on to her stomach, trying to blot out the visions tormenting her, but the unfamiliar ache in her lower body only reinforced what she was trying to ignore.

And then she saw her bedside clock, and realised that the noises she could hear were not just little men with hammers in her head, but were actually coming from downstairs.

She was out of bed before she realised she was naked, and worse, that she had no recollection of how she had got there. As she stood in the middle of her bedroom floor, trying to ignore the nauseous feeling in her stomach and the awful taste in her mouth, she heard someone knock on her bedroom door. She only just had time to dive back into bed and to pull the covers up to her chin before Oliver walked in.

Her mouth dropped open as she saw him. He looked so calm, so unaffected by what had happened.

'The plumber has deputed me to tell you that the water's off and likely to remain off for most of the day,' he told her cheerfully, before putting a mug of coffee beside the bed. 'I brought this as a peace offering.'

No water. But she had to get showered and dressed and off to work. She had several appointments, including one with Dan Pearce.

Watching the expressions haunting her face, Oliver silently cursed. He should have woken her earlier, talked to her, but he had wanted to create the right setting, the right mood in which she would listen to him.

'Charlotte, about last night.'

Charlotte's head came up. She glared at him, filled with self-contempt and loathing. Oh, God, what had she done? Now he was going to tell her that last night had been a mistake, that it was something they should both forget. Her stomach churned. She was going to be sick, she recognised helplessly.

'I don't want to talk about it,' she told him through tight lips. 'And, unless you get a kick out of watching people be sick, I'd rather you went away.'

'Sick? You feel sick? Wait.'

'I can't wait,' Charlotte told him grimly, frantically wrenching the sheet off the bed, and somehow managing to wrap it around herself as she almost fell out of bed and ran for the bathroom.

Of course there was no water, other than that already in the taps, and, grimacing to herself as she tried to clean her teeth with half a glass of water, she wondered what on earth this already doomed day could possibly have in store.

Back in her bedroom, the smell of the coffee nauseated her, but she forced herself to drink it, while she dressed in clean clothes, wondering desperately why on earth the expensive French scent Sheila had given her for Christmas did nothing to blot out the subtle smell of Oliver's body on her own.

She had half expected him to be waiting for her downstairs, wanting to reinforce the fact that last night had been some kind of mental aberration on both their parts and, as such, best forgotten.

Forgotten... She groaned to herself as she walked into the kitchen. How could she ever forget... when she had made such a fool of herself...? How could she have ever been stupid enough to think that...?

That what? That his desire had matched her own, that he had wanted her in all the ways she had wanted him, that he loved her in the way she loved him.

Fool indeed. And she had no one to blame for that folly but herself. She had been the one to initiate their intimacy, to let him see that she wanted him, to invite him virtually to make love to her...

As she walked into the kitchen, the plumber, whom she had not seen before, looked up and grunted. 'Your husband said to tell you he'd be back in half an hour, missus.'

Her husband... Hysterical laughter bubbled up inside her. Laughter or tears—neither of them would really relieve the pain inside her.

Ignoring the plumber and the other men, Charlotte opened the door and headed for her car. Heaven alone knew what Sheila must be thinking. She had already missed her first appointment this morning.

It was only after she had narrowly avoided a collision with another motorist that she realised how recklessly she was driving. As recklessly as she had behaved last night. What was it... this unfamiliar recklessness tormenting her? Was it caused by the knowledge that her love for Oliver would never be reciprocated, that he could never feel for her what she felt for him?

She wondered if, when she returned this evening, she would find that he had moved out, and laughed bitterly at her own thoughts. She was only surprised that he had still been there this morning.

When she walked into her office half an hour later, her scalp was tight with tension; hypersensitively she wondered if Sheila would be as acutely aware of the changes within her as she was herself, but, apart from giving her a brief smile, Sheila seemed unaware of anything different about her.

'Oliver rang to warn us you'd be late in,' she said cheerfully, 'so I sent Sophy over to show the Bramwells round number fourteen. She should be back soon.'

Charlotte managed to conceal her shock. 'What exactly did Oliver say?' she asked cautiously, when she felt she could.

'Oh, just that the two of you had celebrated something together last night and indulged rather too heavily in vintage champagne.' Sheila grinned at her. 'Don't think I don't sympathise. There's nothing worse than a hangover. What *were* you celebrating, by the way?' Sheila asked her speculatively. 'Or shouldn't I ask?'

All too conscious of the hot tide of colour burning her skin, Charlotte dipped her head and said unevenly, 'Nothing much. Oliver's sold out his agency in London and decided to base himself permanently here.'

'Mmm. Cause for celebration indeed,' Sheila murmured thoughtfully, her glance resting for a moment on Charlotte's downbent head, a small smile curving her mouth. 'You've resigned yourself to it, then?' she asked innocently.

Immediately Charlotte's head shot up. 'To what?'

'To Oliver's being here,' Sheila responded.

'I don't seem to have much option, do I?' Charlotte told her grittily. For a moment, she had actually thought that Sheila must know—but how could she? She was allowing her own feelings of remorse and self-contempt to colour everything she heard.

She was thankful to escape from the office and from Sheila's searching gaze to keep her appointment with Dan Pearce, even though she was not really looking forward to dealing with him. She didn't like the man at all. There was something about him . . .

Telling herself not to be so stupid, Charlotte got in her car and drove out in the direction of the farm. She had arranged to meet Dan Pearce at the cottages he was hoping to sell, and when she drew up outside them to find his battered Land Rover already there she suppressed a pang of disquiet.

There was no sign of the farmer outside the property, and so she opened the door to the first semi and walked in, calling his name. She could hear sounds of someone moving about upstairs and she put her hand on the worn handrail and went to investigate. She found the farmer in the first of the poky, stuffy bedrooms and realised as she approached the window that he must have watched her drive up. She frowned, recognising that he had made no attempt to come down and meet her, her unfamiliar feeling of disquiet growing as he turned round and leered at her.

'Came, then, did you?' he said to her. 'That's what you're like, though, isn't it, you women? Once you get a taste for it.'

Alarm bells were ringing in Charlotte's brain. Instinctively she stepped back towards the door, but he moved faster, trapping her in the room as he closed the door and stood in front of it.

Fear knifed through her—the kind of fear she had never known could exist, the kind of fear she had deliberately closed her eyes to, just as she always preferred not to read about accounts of her sex being frightened and abused in the way that she now sensed this man wanted to frighten and abuse her.

Rape. Such a short but ugly word. A word she had never really focused on.

She tried to tell herself she was being foolish, over-imaginative, that she had misunderstood what he had said, and what he had left unsaid, but nothing could banish the panic now clawing inside her.

She tried to think, to stay calm, to lift herself past the fear blocking her ability to think and reason.

'You wanted to discuss selling the cottages as a single unit, Mr Pearce,' she said as firmly as she could. 'I think that's a sensible decision. Of course, planning permission would have——'

She heard him laugh and any hopes she might have had that she was mistaken, that he was not deliberately trying to intimidate her, that he had not brought her here for a purpose that had nothing to do with his property died.

As she stared into his unpleasant, over-confident, leering face, a feeling of intense dread washed over her. She looked desperately at the door, wondering if she could risk running past him, if she could take him off guard sufficiently for her to pull open the door, and then she saw the way he was grinning at her and she knew he was waiting for her to do just that very thing, so that he could have the pleasure of punishing her for it, and she shuddered in open revulsion.

Dear God, how had this happened? *Why* had she not realised? Sheila had warned her...or tried to...

Fear twisted and coiled inside her like a live thing, writhing, burning, making her want to be sick, to scream, to beat her fists against the walls entrapping her, to plead and beg for her freedom.

Fighting desperately not to give in to her panic, she said huskily, 'Mr Pearce, it seems that we are both under a misapprehension. I thought you asked me here to discuss the sale of these houses.'

He was laughing openly at her now. 'No, you didn't,' he told her. 'You know what I want from you. I told you last time you was here I wasn't going to sell 'em together. Like I said, living with that Londoner's given you a taste for it. All the same, your sort—all airs and graces outside, but inside you're no better than whores, leading a man on. Just the same as that whore I married. She was like you.'

He was mad, Charlotte thought frantically. He must be if he thought that she had actually encouraged him to believe... Where before it had been the sexual assault of her body she had feared, now she felt a sharp thrill of horror. He could rape and then murder her. No one would know. No one could help her.

As she watched him watching her, anticipating her pain, enjoying her panic, she had a fierce sensation of triumph that she had had last night—that whatever happened she had at least those memories of her time with Oliver to use as a shield against whatever this man might try to do to her.

She was afraid, yes—desperately so—but just thinking about Oliver, just remembering the pleasure he had given her, somehow steadied her and subdued her panic so that her brain started to work again, urging her to keep on talking to him, to try to distract him.

'I'm afraid I don't know what you're trying to imply,' she said as frigidly as she could, adding, 'I don't have a lot of time, Mr Pearce. I have another appointment in half an hour. In fact, my assistant will soon be wondering where I am, if I don't return to the office.'

It wasn't entirely untrue. She did have another appointment, but not for an hour. And in an hour...

'You're lying,' he told her savagely. 'But it won't work. You came here because you're just like all the rest.'

Charlotte tried desperately to blot out the words that spewed from his sick mind, to ignore and deny the horror of what he was threatening to do to her. He must have been like this since his wife had left him, she recognised, wondering with another thrill of horror how many other women he might have subjected to the same ordeal he was now inflicting on her.

The air in the small room was stale, putrid almost, or was that her imagination? His hands were filthy, his nails broken and black; she cringed visualising them on her skin. Nausea built up inside her. She couldn't endure much more. Her self-control was cracking already.

'If you're not prepared to discuss the sale of these properties, then I'm afraid I must leave,' she told him, trying to appear confident, as she stepped towards the door.

For a moment she thought she had succeeded, and that he would simply let her go. He actually let her reach the door, stepping aside for her, and she was trembling as she touched the handle, relief flooding her. He had simply been testing her, frightening her. Her legs felt weak, her mouth dry.

And then, just as she turned the handle, he grabbed hold of her, turning her round and slamming her back against the door. The pain winded her, depriving her of the ability to even scream in protest.

She could feel his hot breath on her face, could feel the painful bite of his fingers through her clothes. Oh, God, why hadn't she stayed where she was?

'Like it a bit rough, do you?' she heard him saying thickly. 'Like being messed around a bit, like? My wife was like that. Oh, she used to scream and cry and pretend she hated it, but I knew different.'

Charlotte shuddered as she listened to him, all too easily picturing the other woman's agony. How on earth had she endured her marriage? No wonder she had left him.

'Yes, she liked it so much she used to claw at my back and beg me.'

Charlotte couldn't help it. She covered her ears with her hands and screamed helplessly. 'Stop it! Stop it!'

It was a mistake. Her stomach lurched as she realised that her panic was only exciting him, inciting him to gaze boldly at her body, his eyes hot, his fingers kneading her flesh where he held her as he focused on her breasts...

How long had she been here? How long would her ordeal last? She dared not even risk looking at her watch. Suddenly, terrifyingly, she wanted it to be over, and illuminatingly she could quite easily see why his wife had allowed him the possession of her body. It was simply easier not to fight, to allow him what he wanted and to get it over with.

Shudder after shudder racked through her as he watched her gloatingly, telling her what he intended to do with her. With every word he was becoming more excited, more unrestrained.

He was confusing her with his wife, Charlotte recognised sickly, as he called her 'Marlene' not once but twice.

In another few minutes she would be unconscious. She could feel her strength ebbing, her body aching for the release from what was happening. Her head was spinning.

And then unbelievably she heard Oliver calling her name, and thought dazedly that she had actually slipped over the edge and was unconscious until Dan Pearce suddenly clamped his filthy hand over

her mouth and said, 'Don't try and say a word.
He'll not come up here. No once he realises you
want to be with me.'

Stupidly Charlotte stared at him, worn out with
terror and pain, and then abruptly she realised that
Oliver actually *was* there, that he actually had come
looking for her, that he actually was calling her
name, and with a strength she hadn't known she
had she struggled against her captor, sinking her
teeth sharply into his palm, long enough to draw
air into her lungs and to scream Oliver's name
before Dan Pearce grabbed hold of her hair and
slammed her head back against the door, yelling
out, 'She wants me, not you. She's nothing but a
whore, who'll open her legs for anyone. They're all
the same.'

Charlotte heard the words, but only distantly.
Her head hurt; she felt sick and dizzy. There was
something warm and sticky running down her face
and someone seemed to be kicking her back. The
kicking ceased abruptly when the door flew open
and she was thrown to the floor. She heard herself
scream as she fell, and then everything went black,
although she was dimly conscious of someone
touching her, soothing her, speaking to her.
Someone whom it was important she reached out
to... only it was all too much of an effort.

She had been having a very bad dream, Charlotte
recognised, opening her eyes. Her bedroom was in
darkness, but its outline was familiar. So why had
she confused it with somewhere else... a hospital?

And why had she woken up so often crying for Oliver, wanting desperately to be held by him, to be safe with him?

Her head was aching. She put up her hand to touch it, wincing at the pain in her shoulder and then frowning as her fingers touched the plaster she found.

Confusing memories stirred sluggishly. Images that haunted her bad dreams... fragments of sensation... of fear... 'No!'

'Charlotte, it's all right. You're quite safe.'

She lay still, her heart pounding frantically in the darkness. What was Oliver doing in bed with her? Had she gone completely crazy? Was she perhaps imagining...? But no. Impossible to imagine the tenderness of those hands touching her, turning her, drawing her into the warmth of his body, patting her back as though soothing a terrified child.

'Oliver... what are you doing here?' Her voice sounded rusty and strained.

'You wanted me with you... remember?'

She wrinkled her forehead. She did have an odd hazy memory of crying out for him. That had been when she was in the hospital, hadn't it? And suddenly her body went hot as she realised she must actually have been there, that others must actually have heard her...

'It's all right,' Oliver was reassuring her, as though he had read her mind. 'No one was shocked or surprised. I told them you were my fiancée and in the circumstances they could quite understand why you should want to be with me. That was the only reason they let me bring you home.'

'Because you said you'd sleep with me?' she questioned warily. 'But——'

'Oh, Sheila and I practically came to blows over who should take charge of you,' he told her. 'In the end it was the way you clung to me that persuaded the hospital staff that you should come with me. You'll be pleased to know that there'll be no lasting damage—at least not of the physical variety. A very unpleasant-looking collection of bruises, and a nasty bash on the head, which was the reason they kept you in in the first place.'

Abruptly she remembered. She trembled in his arms as she said stiltedly, 'He didn't touch me. Not...not in that way. He was going to. He thought I was his wife.'

'Shush...we know all about it. He was a very dangerous man. A very sick man mentally.'

'I should never have gone there. I knew inside that there was something about him.' She twisted in his arms. 'I wanted to sell those houses so that you wouldn't get them. I never thought... It could have been Sophy!' she burst out frantically. 'I could have sent Sophy.'

She started to cry. Deep, wrenching sobs that tore at his heart and made him wish he had had just half a dozen minutes alone with her attacker before the police had arrived.

It had been Sheila who had alerted him to her potential danger. When he had discovered that she had gone to work without waiting to see him, he had driven in too and gone into the office, only to find Sheila already concerned. A chance call from someone who had already approached Dan Pearce with an offer to buy both semis from him at a fair market price and had been turned down flat had revealed to her that, whatever the farmer's reason for luring Charlotte out to the deserted building, it could have had nothing to do with any change of heart about selling the two units as one.

She had poured out her concern to Oliver, and he had promptly offered to drive over to the buildings to check that Charlotte was all right.

Once he had gone, Sheila's fears had increased and she had rung her husband, asking him to check as well, hence the police's arrival within seconds of Oliver's having broken down the door and discovered Charlotte unconscious on the floor, her blouse ripped, bruises already forming on her bare shoulders.

For a moment he had suffered a blind, fierce need to destroy the man standing over her, to rip him limb from limb, but, just as sanity was reasserting itself and he was forcing himself to recognise that his first task must be to get Charlotte away to safety, the police had arrived and taken charge.

He didn't want to tell her yet about the gun that Dan Pearce had somehow or other got his hands on when the police had taken him back to the farmhouse, nor the fact that he had taken his own life with it. That could come later...

It had torn him apart to learn from the hospital that she was crying for him in her sleep. And, indeed, the moment he had walked up to her bed and taken hold of her hand she had become calmer.

Now she had been at home for almost forty-eight hours, although she had been so heavily sedated at first that she would have no memory of her return. Last night he had slept with her in his arms, soothing her nightmares, comforting and cherishing her, and he would continue to do so for the rest of his life if that was what she wanted.

'You should have let me go with Sheila,' she told him shakily. 'Now the whole town will know we're supposed to engaged, and when they learn that we aren't——'

'Need they?'

His question stunned her. She tensed, and missed the warmth of his hands on her back as he removed them to frame her face so that she couldn't avoid his searching study of her features.

'Yes...unless you intend to carry this farce as far as marriage,' she said fiercely.

'Willingly. But to me it isn't a farce, only the realisation of a need that was born in me the first time we met.'

She stared at him in disbelief. 'When Vanessa introduced us? You can't mean that.'

'I don't. Our first meeting was in the car park, when you stole my parking spot. I saw you, watched you, knew that I should have been furious with you, and yet all I wanted to do was to get out of my car, take you in my arms and tell you that I'd fallen in love with you.'

Charlotte looked at him, searching his face for some sign that he was making it all up, but there was none.

'I've done everything the wrong way round. I wanted to do this slowly, properly—to win your confidence and then your love.'

'And that's why you plied me with champagne and made love to me?' she asked shakily. A tender hope was growing quickly inside her.

'That wasn't my intention. Oh, I wanted to make love to you all right. But I wasn't going to—at least, only a little, but then you looked at me and asked me if I wanted to, and all I'd been able to think about all day was the sight of you in that damned flimsy cotton thing, and—— Oh, God, Charlotte, how you could *ever* for one moment have imagined that you lacked sex appeal, I have no idea. You were the sexiest sight I have ever seen, all the more so because you yourself were so deliciously unaware of the effect you were having on me. Every time I saw you, I had to fight to keep my hands off you.'

'But no man has ever——'

'Because you wouldn't let them see what you were really like. Because you froze them off and they, poor fools, couldn't see the real woman you were concealing behind those barriers you used so effectively.'

'Not all of them,' Charlotte told him in a low voice, and he knew she wasn't referring to him.

'He was sick,' he told her rawly. 'You must never think that it was something you said or did. It was because of his wife.'

'I know,' Charlotte admitted. 'Oh, God, I was so frightened.' Suddenly it all came pouring out, a catharsis of what she had experienced, her need to share it with him so intense that nothing could dam up the words. 'And do you know what I thought when I felt it was unavoidable that he *would* rape and probably murder me?'

Oliver shook his head, aching to hold her as tightly as he could, but terrified of hurting her...or frightening her.

'I was glad that there'd been you,' she told him simply. 'So very glad and grateful, because you'd shown me such pleasure, such...'

'Such love,' he said for her. His throat felt raw with emotion, and when he wrapped her in his arms he knew she would feel his tears against her skin. 'Oh, God, Charlotte. I've been cursing myself to hell and back for that, loathing myself for not having the self-control to wait, to talk to you, to tell you how I felt about you first. I did everything wrong. I wanted to be with you when you woke up, but those damned workmen were there. And then you were so sick; you looked so ill. I thought I'd drive into town and get you something from the chemist. It never occurred to me that you'd just go straight to work.'

'I had to. I thought you were going to say the usual thing about its being something we should both forget, that we should behave like adults.'

'*Is* that the usual thing?'

She could hear the amusement in his voice and said defensively, 'Well, you know what I mean. I didn't dare hope that you might love me. You see, all my life my father let me know how unsatisfactory he found me as a daughter...as a woman——'

'Yes, I know,' Oliver interrupted her gently. 'Sheila told me. Parents can do such appalling damage to their children, but you are a woman, Charlotte—the only woman, as far as I'm concerned. A very, very desirable and desired woman, whom I love very much. If you can love me too, that's all I ask. This experience you've had...traumatic for any woman——'

She knew what he was going to say and gently shook her head.

'No. It was frightening, terrifyingly so, but luckily you came in time, before he could do anything more than simply tell me what he wanted to do to me, and somehow I think the knowledge of what I'd shared with you isolated me from the real horror of it. It was as though nothing he could say or do to me could come between me and the memories you'd given me. I'm not afraid to make love again, Oliver,' she told him gravely, and then froze as he said wryly,

'I am.'

He saw from her face that she had misunderstood him, and cursed her father silently. How long would it be before she accepted that she *was* desirable in every single sense of the word?

'I don't want our first child to be conceived outside our marriage,' he told her firmly, 'and I don't want to wait any longer than I have to to make you my wife. Will you marry me, my darling?'

Sheila was delighted when they told her, as much by Charlotte's unexpected and heart-warmingly open admission that, since Oliver refused to make love to her until they were married, she wanted the ceremony to take place just as soon as it could be arranged, as by the actual announcement of their engagement.

'Of course, you know the only reason he's marrying me is so that he can get his hands on the business,' she teased.

They would merge the two businesses, of course; she would continue to work—for the time being at least. She had found she was daydreaming increasingly frequently of those two dark-blue-eyed children.

Since neither of them had any close family, the ceremony they planned was to be a quiet, simple one, which was what they both wanted.

The day before they were due to be married, Oliver returned home late in the afternoon and found Charlotte sitting in the orchard under the old apple tree. She was almost asleep, and, when she opened her eyes and saw him, she smiled lazily at him.

'I was just daydreaming about how I felt when you made love to me here.' She saw the way his eyes darkened, and laughed softly. 'You were the one who imposed the ban,' she reminded him, and then whispered wickedly, 'We're going to be married tomorrow—in less than twenty-four hours.' She patted the grass beside her coaxingly and heard him groan.

There was laughter in her eyes as well as desire as he came down beside her and she whispered in his ear, 'Thank goodness for that. For a moment I thought I was going to have to resort to this.'

Behind her, nestling in the grass, was a bottle of champagne with two glasses.

Oliver laughed with her as he rolled her beneath him but, when he kissed her, for both of them the laughter was stilled.

'This is when we make our vows to one another,' Charlotte told him huskily. 'This is when we make the promises that we'll never break. Make love to me, Oliver.'

'All the days of my life,' he promised huskily. 'All the days of my life.'

HARLEQUIN

Romance

A Christmas tradition...

Imagine spending Christmas in New
Orleans with a blind stranger and his aged
guide dog—when you're supposed to be
there on your honeymoon!
#3163 Every Kind of Heaven
by Bethany Campbell

Imagine spending Christmas with a man
you once "married"—in a mock ceremony
at the age of eight!
#3166 The Forgetful Bride
by Debbie Macomber

*Available in December 1991, wherever
Harlequin books are sold.*

HARLEQUIN
PROUDLY PRESENTS
A DAZZLING NEW CONCEPT IN ROMANCE FICTION

One small town—twelve terrific love stories

Welcome to Tyler, Wisconsin—a town full of people
you'll enjoy getting to know, memorable friends and
unforgettable lovers, and a long-buried secret that
lurks beneath its serene surface....

JOIN US FOR A YEAR IN THE LIFE OF TYLER

Each book set in Tyler is a self-contained love story;
together, the twelve novels stitch the fabric of a
community.

LOSE YOUR HEART TO TYLER!

The excitement begins in March 1992, with
WHIRLWIND, by Nancy Martin. When lively, brash
Liza Baron arrives home unexpectedly, she moves
into the old family lodge, where the silent and
mysterious Cliff Forrester has been living in seclusion
for years....

WATCH FOR ALL TWELVE BOOKS
OF THE TYLER SERIES
Available wherever Harlequin books are sold

TYLER-G

"INDULGE A LITTLE" SWEEPSTAKES

HERE'S HOW THE SWEEPSTAKES WORKS

NO PURCHASE NECESSARY

To enter each drawing, complete the appropriate Official Entry Form or a 3" by 5" index card by hand-printing your name, address and phone number and the trip destination that the entry is being submitted for (i.e., Walt Disney World Vacation Drawing, etc.) and mailing it to: Indulge '91 Subscribers-Only Sweepstakes, P.O. Box 1397, Buffalo, New York 14269-1397.

No responsibility is assumed for lost, late or misdirected mail. Entries must be sent separately with first class postage affixed, and be received by: 9/30/91 for the Walt Disney World Vacation Drawing, 10/31/91 for the Alaskan Cruise Drawing and 11/30/91 for the Hawaiian Vacation Drawing. Sweepstakes is open to residents of the U.S. and Canada, 21 years of age or older as of 11/7/91.

For complete rules, send a self-addressed, stamped (WA residents need not affix return postage) envelope to: Indulge '91 Subscribers-Only Sweepstakes Rules, P.O. Box 4005, Blair, NE 68009.

© 1991 HARLEQUIN ENTERPRISES LTD.   DIR-RL

- -

"INDULGE A LITTLE" SWEEPSTAKES

HERE'S HOW THE SWEEPSTAKES WORKS

NO PURCHASE NECESSARY

To enter each drawing, complete the appropriate Official Entry Form or a 3" by 5" index card by hand-printing your name, address and phone number and the trip destination that the entry is being submitted for (i.e., Walt Disney World Vacation Drawing, etc.) and mailing it to: Indulge '91 Subscribers-Only Sweepstakes, P.O. Box 1397, Buffalo, New York 14269-1397.

No responsibility is assumed for lost, late or misdirected mail. Entries must be sent separately with first class postage affixed, and be received by: 9/30/91 for the Walt Disney World Vacation Drawing, 10/31/91 for the Alaskan Cruise Drawing and 11/30/91 for the Hawaiian Vacation Drawing. Sweepstakes is open to residents of the U.S. and Canada, 21 years of age or older as of 11/7/91.

For complete rules, send a self-addressed, stamped (WA residents need not affix return postage) envelope to: Indulge '91 Subscribers-Only Sweepstakes Rules, P.O. Box 4005, Blair, NE 68009.

© 1991 HARLEQUIN ENTERPRISES LTD.   DIR-RL

INDULGE A LITTLE—WIN A LOT!

Summer of '91 Subscribers-Only Sweepstakes

OFFICIAL ENTRY FORM

This entry must be received by: Nov. 30, 1991
This month's winner will be notified by: Dec. 7, 1991
Trip must be taken between: Jan. 7, 1992—Jan. 7, 1993

YES, I want to win the 3-Island Hawaiian vacation for two. I understand the prize includes round-trip airfare, first-class hotels and pocket money as revealed on the "wallet" scratch-off card.

Name _____

Address _____ Apt. _____

City _____

State/Prov. _____ Zip/Postal Code _____

Daytime phone number _____
(Area Code)

Return entries with invoice in envelope provided. Each book in this shipment has two entry coupons—and the more coupons you enter, the better your chances of winning!

© 1991 HARLEQUIN ENTERPRISES LTD.   3R-CPS

INDULGE A LITTLE—WIN A LOT!

Summer of '91 Subscribers-Only Sweepstakes

OFFICIAL ENTRY FORM

This entry must be received by: Nov. 30, 1991
This month's winner will be notified by: Dec. 7, 1991
Trip must be taken between: Jan. 7, 1992—Jan. 7, 1993

YES, I want to win the 3-Island Hawaiian vacation for two. I understand the prize includes round-trip airfare, first-class hotels and pocket money as revealed on the "wallet" scratch-off card.

Name _____

Address _____ Apt. _____

City _____

State/Prov. _____ Zip/Postal Code _____

Daytime phone number _____
(Area Code)

Return entries with invoice in envelope provided. Each book in this shipment has two entry coupons—and the more coupons you enter, the better your chances of winning!

© 1991 HARLEQUIN ENTERPRISES LTD.   3R-CPS